ID0638501

Edited by John Metcalf

Best Canadian Stories
13

LONDON PUBLIC LIBRARY

Copyright © 2013 by Oberon Press

ALL RIGHTS RESERVED

The publishers acknowledge the support of the Canada Council for the Arts, the Government of Ontario through the Ontario Media Development Corporation and the Government of Canada through the Canada Book Fund for their publishing activities.

"The Amaretto" by Valerie Spencer first appeared in *Fiddlehead*; "You Know How I Feel" by Elisabeth de Mariaffi first appeared in *Fiddlehead* and was included in *How To Get Along With Women* (Invisible Publishing); "Ellen-Celine, Celine-Ellen" by Caroline Adderson was originally published in *Canadian Notes & Queries*, and won the National Magazine Awards gold medal for fiction; "The Everpresent Hell of Other People" by Marjorie Celona was first published in *Harvard Review*; "The Land Below" by Alice Petersen was originally published in *Room*; "Addresses" by Cynthia Flood first appeared at FoundPress.com; "The Fires of Soweto" by Heather Davidson and "Sleep World" by Zoey Leigh Peterson were first published in *The New Quarterly*, and "Sleep World" was shortlisted for the Journey Prize.

The following magazines were consulted: *The Antigonish Review, The Capilano Review, The Danforth Review, Descant, Event, Exile, The Fiddlehead, Geist, Grain, The Malahat Review, Matrix, The New Quarterly, Prairie Fire, PRISM international* and *subTerrain*.

ISBN 978 0 7780 1402 7 (hardcover)
ISBN 978 0 7780 1403 4 (softcover)
ISSN 0703 9476

Cover art by Alexej von Jawlensky
Book design by Michael Macklem
Printed in Canada

PUBLISHED IN CANADA BY OBERON PRESS

Canada Council   Conseil des Arts
for the Arts   du Canada

Contributions for the forty-fourth volume, published or unpublished, should be sent to Oberon Press, 205–145 Spruce Street, Ottawa, Ontario K1R 6P1 before 31 March, 2014. All manuscripts should enclose a stamped self-addressed envelope.

The stories this year in the forty-third edition of *Best Canadian Stories* surprised me as much as they will surprise you. Four of the stories are the first appearances in book form for their authors—Valerie Spencer, Kathryn Mulvihill, Heather Davidson, and Zoey Leigh Peterson. Where do they come from and how are they so accomplished at the very beginnings of careers? I am astonished at the comic sparkle of Valerie Spencer, the sure and subtle hand of Zoey Leigh Peterson. Kathryn Mulvihill's imagination is working towards enshrining a time and place, an anglo enclave across the river from Ottawa in the Gatineau. Heather Davidson's "The Fires of Soweto" is touched and flushed by poetic power.

The middle ground is by writers, who, subsequent to their selection here, recently published a first book. Elisabeth de Mariaffi (*How to Get Along with Women*), Alice Petersen (*All the Voices Cry*), and Marjorie Celona (the novel, *Y*).

And then there are the…(I was about to commit the cliché "grizzled veterans" but immediately suppressed it as being possibly unwise)…the *stalwarts* of Canadian short fiction writing, Caroline Adderson, Clark Blaise, Cynthia Flood, and Patricia Robertson.

Last year I selected Caroline Adderson's "Poppycock", this year "Ellen-Celine, Celine-Ellen"; Caroline's stories are full house, always moving and often deadpan funny. Cynthia Flood's stories, gritty, often painful, grip us with a reality from which we cannot turn. Patricia Robertson's last two collections *City of Orphans* and *The Goldfish Dancer* range over North Africa, Spain, northern England, a prairie detention centre in First World War Canada, and the medieval Arab world, stories subtle and plangent. Clark Blaise has revealed himself over the years as one of our finest and most important writers. "We Are All Illegals" swells the portrait he painted in his collection, *The Meagre Tarmac*, of the East-Indian/American world in California, a world of young high-achievers and parents the inheritors of implacable tradition.

I'm sometimes asked how I pick these stories, how I recognize them—*Aren't your choices and judgements purely subjective?*

Yes, absolutely and joyously.

Recently I'm returned from a holiday in Rome. There are twenty-two or twenty-three Caravaggio paintings in Rome in national collections housed in the Borghese, Barberini, Corsini, and Pamphilj palazzos, and in the churches which commissioned them for their chapels. I visited them all.

The church interiors are usually tenebrous. Through the gloom one can make out Depositions, Pietas, Dormitions, Martyrdoms, Flights into Egypt—acres of conventional paint until suddenly, a trumpet blast in the mouldering silence, *there* is a Caravaggio. One doesn't have to search for them. They proclaim themselves.

Just as these stories do.

They pick *me*.

JOHN METCALF

The Amaretto
Valerie Spencer

In the cool morning air, Willy Tingle slips into yesterday's boxer shorts, size large but dainty in a way, patterned with French horns and undulating banners that read *Happy Anniversary, Happy Anniversary*. He tiptoes toward the bedroom door, away from the unforgiving orthopaedic mattress where his wife of 30 years lies puttering little snores into the soft skin at the crook of her arm. In the upstairs hall, he holds his breath as the bottom of the door carves a rough, noisy arc into the broadloom and is ssshut.

Willy loves his wife, but an early morning without her can be the best part of his weekend. And he knows that Janice will not be happy this morning. She is probably unhappy right now, in her sleep. And making a plan.

Downstairs in the kitchen, Willy runs a few inches of tepid tap water into the kettle and fishes his mug from a pile of dishes in the sink. He makes instant coffee, adds milk and a dash of paprika, his secret ingredient, secret at least since his wife had told him what she thought of the idea. He picks over last night's little sandwiches, all of which smell like tuna paste and slump with the leaking fruit on aluminum party trays. Sandwiches and mug in hand, he wanders from room to room, taking measure of his hospitality. Half-full glasses, soggy paper plates, shoes— whose? A bottle of amaretto and a ukulele in the laundry-room.

The party had been Janice's idea. She'd announced it two months ago, right after a long, one-sided phone call from Fiona Finklemarr, whose husband saluted their fourteenth wedding anniversary with an outside cabin on a cruise ship to Bulgaria. "Romanian girls tan topless, you know, and when one is in

9

Rome..." Fiona said.

"A *big* party Willy," Janice said.

In the kitchen once again, he begins to scrape condiments and cake from the plates. He doesn't mind kitchen duty, thinks the kitchen a great place. He likes the mystery of leftovers, surprises in blue plastic bowls and old cookie tins. Just the once, he found a part bottle of good scotch under the sink, right there with the steel wool and the ant bait. He likes the gadgets in the middle drawer, the endless shapes and working parts—wires, rollers, cogs, mesh, pins, bulbs—it's like having a whole drawer full of answers, he says. He likes how dishwater with baking soda and a rag can do almost anything if you are patient. At Christmas, he'd spent two hours shining the steel kettle and big hanging spoons and the chrome knobs on the cupboards, until the room sang with tiny upside-down trees, flashing red-green, in series.

It's not that Willy is averse to parties. We have our share, he'd told Janice. Modest parties for modest people, he'd said (she was icy for the rest of the day). And it's not that he ignores their wedding anniversary. The first time that Willy stripped down to the shorts with the French horns and banners, Janice was tickled. He'd knelt to present her with a pair of earrings, little wooden balls for the fifth, and asked her to marry him all over again. They'd had a wonderful night. Every year since, he got the boxers out from the back of his drawer for the fun of it, and gave her jewellery—a slender, iron bracelet for their sixth, a silk flower pendant at twelve and crystal earrings for fifteen years. He took her out to dinner. Just the two of them. Even now, after 30 years, when there is no elastic left in the shorts and none needed, he couldn't wait to propose, get down on one knee, give her the new brooch—two pearl peas in a silver pod—and hear her say "Yes."

Janice is not a person easily bent to "yes." She leans to "yes but if only." We don't live in a bubble, she says, coming home with new high-heeled boots and a sample book of wallpaper. Most people notice these things, she says, when Willy forgets to hang the six-foot, musical wreath on the garage. Janice makes lists, leaves notes everywhere in her practiced, exquisite handwriting, so much To Do, Today, and oh, she sees the possibilities knit together magically on paper. She loves the chase of this season's sources and last season's sales—shoes, shrubs and kitchen gadgets, how-to books, go-to gurus and the fabulous faux. She can window shop for hours, looking for this but looking at that. It's hard work, seeing the possibilities. When she is overtired or outdone, she turns her frustration outward, keeps from feeling downhearted by making plans. Janice can pick through the small events of that day or several days, her critical eye turned to the sweet moments that should not have been lost and to the sour bits that keep adding up. When crossed, she can nurture a fledgling grudge through the awkward stage, when other people might be persuaded to drop it in embarrassment.

Bingo! Under a tinfoil tent, Willy finds a dozen Swedish meatballs congealed in position around a pineapple ring. The layout puts him in mind of a hockey play (some idiot has thrown parsley onto the ice) and he does a little skate around the kitchen with the tray of meatballs, munching on the players, beginning with defence and thinking Pittsburgh. He is three meatballs from the blue line when a bout of sneezing and the hollow thunk of a body falling hard against the refrigerator door announce the entrance of a grey Scottish terrier with arthritic haunches and the brow line of Albert Einstein. Collapsed by the fridge, Bruce seems to be asleep. Then a tiny, primal place in the dog's brain connects to the tray in Willy's hands. Rocking and wheezing, Bruce gains enough momentum to hoist hindquarters and lurch forward, afoot if not alert. Willy is reluctant to forfeit the last of his leftovers but agrees with Bruce that an early morning showdown would be humiliating to both of them. He stuffs the remaining meatballs with the dog's vitamins and thyroid pill.

Bruce has snuffled off into the hallway when Janice appears. Willy is at the sink, running hot water, singing under his breath (*G-L-O-R-I-A...Glow ree ah.*). He's tied a pastry apron over his boxer shorts. Pale, hairy nipples peek from either side of the bib as he turns to his wife, smiling, encouraging, good morning my love. Janice is wearing a sullen face and a sapphire blue nightgown made of the sheerest chiffon. Her terry bathrobe is open, its belt dragging on the floor. While she takes silent stock of the kitchen, Willy looks through the filmy fabric at his wife's breasts and legs and panties. She always wears panties to bed.

White cotton panties as big as placemats, and delicate, diaphanous nighties, with plunging necklines and thin straps that won't stay up. Last night she'd slept in bobby pins and a scarf to keep her hair piled high on her head, away from the pillow. Beautiful. This is what the Queen looks like when she wakes up, Willy thinks. Janice has bare feet and a corn plaster. Willy wants to take her by the hand and lead her to the sofa and begin with kissing her poor, plastered foot. She will resist and he will coo her back into the couch, keeping his eyes on hers until hers close from the steady rubbing of his hand under her nightie, against the panties.

"What a nightmare," Janice says and heads off to the living-room.

The party had begun, as planned, at five o'clock. By half past, Roger Killam, from two doors down, is working his way to the water stained hutch where Willy lined up the whiskey alongside some opened liqueur bottles of the type useful to cocktails with five ingredients. Always the optimist, Willy brings the aging liqueurs up from the basement whenever Janice gets an itch for entertaining. Roger's eyes are already bright. He will install himself at the bar and pass the evening with loud jokes. He will ask if I've ordered a bartender, Willy thinks. Roger slaps Willy hard on the back and puts him in a friendly headlock.

"Anybody here order up a bartender?" Roger asks. "Somebody's gotta let this guy enjoy his own party."

Roger shifts the headlock into a cheery choke hold, roughs up Willy's hair, gets busy with the drinks. Dishevelled and breaking a sweat, his shirt riding out of the back of his trousers, Willy starts for the kitchen but is detoured to the front door by his wife for the sparkling surprise that so-and-so, invited, has shown up and brought a little gift which they shouldn't have. Fiona Finklemarr, who's husband has somehow slipped the noose at the front door and is already heading for the bar, gives Willy a flat-bosomed hug, made painful by a dangling earring shaped like an anchor which grinds into his cheek. Dear god, has she drawn blood? Fiona is a tall, humourless woman, given to bouts of awkward questioning before she succumbs to a third glass of wine and becomes a solitary dancer, her long arms undulating with the grace and solemnity of a manta ray. This evening, she is wearing the anchors and a long purple shawl.

"You must tell me," Fiona says, "how men decide on a gift to thank their faithful wives for 30 years of compromise."

At seven o'clock the party is in full swing. The drinkers have been hard at the bar, the non-drinkers have toured every closet, someone has left already. Music plays over the hubbub of interrupted conversations. In the kitchen, two old friends who volunteered to help with the buffet supper argue about which dish and dip should go where—casseroles appear and are bumped by Sumo rules. Janice has gone upstairs for a break and changed out of her new shoes. Willy doesn't know where to go. The house is full of things that do not belong to him—folding chairs, the buffet table (a rental), bunches of helium balloons and crepe paper streamers that hang from the ceiling, ominous, like giant jelly fish. Three very elderly people sit on the couch, arms crossed, watching television with the sound off. For the third time, Willy asks Janice for an explanation of who's who— You know, Piggets...piglets?...no, just the daughter...those friends of Doris...Doris who?...from the checkout...no, the one that closed...that time we went golfing...this year?...No! With Steve and Edie, five years ago, for heaven's sake, Willy!

At first, Bruce had stayed close to the front door, getting ear rubs and dividing the scents between eat and greet. He'd napped, and he was on time for the first of the accidents that left food on the carpet. But the music is getting louder and he hasn't the stamina to be a party animal. He looks up for a moment and locks eyes with Willy who is caught between one of the elderly and a good friend of Janice's, an avid birder who's been whistling and twerping for ten minutes, his eyes focused on a vanishing point somewhere to the left of Willy's ear. I've got to pee, says Bruce.

Willy takes the dog by the collar—unnecessary but it makes them look like something that shouldn't be interfered with— and heads for the back yard. In the rear hall, the closed door to the laundry-room leaks muffled noise and marijuana. Willy cracks the door enough to sneak a peek. Fiona Finklemarr is sitting on the dryer with her eyes closed, playing *Hey Jude* on the ukulele.

In the back yard, Willy says some encouraging words to

Bruce—they both have unreliable bladders and try to keep each other positive—and while the dog walks the fence, Willy thinks about Fiona's question. Thirty years together. He'd tried to give Janice the pearl brooch while they were dressing but it is still burning a hole in his trouser pocket. I can do more, he thought. Tonight, she'd wanted something big. I have to make her party unforgettable.

He had asked her to marry him so many times over the years. It could be more than that. He will get down on one knee in front of everyone. He will promise her another wedding, another party to renew their vows. It will be perfect.

Willy lets Bruce in the back door and slips upstairs to find the words. He cons Janice to the living-room and puts his hands in the air, waves his guests to attention, everyone please, for a toast. The room begins to settle.

"What should I Dooo?" cries a loud, panicked voice, a woman's voice, and in response Bruce whining and barking. The noises come from down the hall. He never barks says Janice, pushing Willy ahead of her, following him to the laundry-room.

Roger Killam, flushed-faced, one hand to his throat, is holding onto the laundry sink but sinking fast; coughing, choking. Willy grabs the back of Roger's collar and bends him at the waist, over the sink. He slaps Roger hard then harder between the shoulder blades. Again. Again. His red face turning to blue, Roger tries to fight but flails. Willy wrestles him from behind, bends them both over the sink, Willy's face on Roger's back, his arms around Roger's belly in a tight bear hug. Like a weight lifter, Willy makes a low grab and thrust, jerks them both upward, backward, Willy's locked wrists driving into Roger's abdomen. Roger grunts the very last of his air and expels something to rattle in the bottom of the sink. An earring shaped like an anchor. All eyes now to Fiona Finklemarr, whose husband turns on his heel and starts a parade of flustered guests to get their coats. Her purple shawl does not quite cover her long naked torso and little bra. When Willy returns from driving Fiona home, the house is dark, his wife in bed. She turns her back and pulls the covers over her ears.

In the cool morning air, Janice wraps and belts her terry cloth robe, brushes moist crumbs from the seat of the sofa and takes a righteous swipe at some uncooperative throw cushions. She tries to straighten the pleated shade of a table lamp but the harp has been bent, the lamp one of a pair. A face springs to mind—an energetic non-drinker who had to be told not to try to lift the carpet in search of hardwood and who was later caught upstairs, unapologetic, going through the medicine cabinet. Part of the fiasco.

Nothing had gone as planned. Her guests brought guests and were in the mood to bully and bore each other. The bickering in the kitchen delayed dinner and the elderly people were so hungry that they crashed the dessert cart and hijacked a whole cheese ball. Someone kept the music blaring and the drinkers were hoarse from hollering. One of her best friends made a bee-line for the carefully arranged helium balloons and, inhaling the stuff, started a Chipmunks competition among the old folks which only settled down when Janice turned on the TV and made them watch skating. Her new shoes were too tight, her decorations too dull, her husband spent too much of his night with the dog. They hadn't opened the gifts that people brought and Willy got his second wind at some point and had something corny up his sleeve (she could tell) which would be bad (she could tell). All of this before the grand finale.

She'd been composing mental notes while she was in bed, personal notes to be written in fountain pen and sent by mail. She will thank each of her guests, in detail, for helping to make her anniversary the memorable day that it was. She will insist that she and Willy have chosen to forgive the unforgettable event that brought the evening to a swift conclusion. No matter what others might say, the Tingles, she will write, do not believe that anyone meant to make a mockery of marriage.

Dammit! Janice follows her nose to a wide smear of cheese ball on the arm of the sofa. Forgiveness? To hell with forgiveness. What is she supposed to do after she forgives them—apologize to everyone on behalf of everyone else? If people were honest they'd admit that taking the high road only feels good when you've somewhere to take it to, when you're slowing down but not quite stopping to mete out a little forgiveness while you wave "so long." Magnanimous in victory. *That's* what she needs to write about. On really great stationery. The triumph that was her party but they missed it. The Tingles forgive, but what they truly regret is that their guests were caused to leave before they could be part of some perfectly chosen surprise which Janice and Willy had been saving for later in the evening. The inspired finishing touch, understated but just right, and how much they'd looked forward to their good friends being there to share it.

Janice collects the strings of softening balloons from corners of the living-room, gathers them into a large, unwieldy bouquet. She finds a sharp, plastic party pick in a cube of sweating kielbasa and begins to stab. The balloons dance out of her way and she gives up, thwarted. Exploring her injuries, looking for sore spots, Janice rolls up her sleeves and pads down the hall to inspect the insult to her laundry-room. White appliances and wire shelves, a wall calendar with seasonal Scottish Terriers and the timeless spider plant in a wicker basket—not the stuff to inspire lust. And yet they had been here, impatient, so reckless that Roger had opened himself wide. Literally swallowed her.

An uncapped bottle, one of Willy's ancient liqueurs with a shabby label, is sitting on the back of the clothes dryer. Janice runs water until scalding and pours the old liqueur down the drain. The bittersweet aroma of amaretto is transformed by hot water and the deep snifter of a sink, into a heady fog that wafts into her eyes and licks her throat. For an instant, there are pungent possibilities in the laundry-room—intimate echoes on the bare walls, cool metal that thrills a warm, bare back, the danger of discovery and the aftershock of brute force—her Willy part of it now, grappling with Roger, subduing him, saving him. Everyone else deserting.

Willy is staring out of the kitchen window, dish towel in hand, when Janice puts her arms around his middle and doesn't let go.

"Our house is full of the most god-awful balloons," she says. "And one hero. I'm proud of you, Willy."

Where the sun streams in and hits the right place along the wall, Bruce rolls over and huffs in his sleep. He will miss the moment when Janice says "Yes."

Ellen-Celine, Celine-Ellen
Caroline Adderson

So Ellen found herself halfway up the North Shore mountains in a near-empty, perpetually cloud-scarved house, eight months pregnant with her second child. Only 21 and already divorcing. Before the unexpected implosion of her marriage, she and Larry had been living on an island populated by born-again hippies, aging draft dodgers and sundry arty types—potters and poets, furniture makers, weavers of kelp. They'd been passionate members of that very close community (Larry too passionate, it turned out), contributors to its pot lucks and Friday night jams in the tiny island hall, users of its free store and babysitting co-op. If you met somebody on the road on Cordova Island, you stopped and talked for half an hour about your garlic crop and your aura. That's the kind of place it was.

But now when Ellen took her two-year-old daughter Mimi to the park, she felt she was from a far-off country, a land of long-tressed, naked-faced women and bearded, huggy men, she a resident alien among the feather-haired and lycraed North Vancouver natives, all of whom chatted in tight circles around the playground equipment, snubbing her. It was 1983. Mimi teetered then fell on all fours in the sandbox. Watching from a nearby bench, Ellen marvelled at how she simply thrust her diapered bottom in the air and boosted herself up. "How do you do that?" she asked, for she, Ellen, was in mid-collapse and would never, ever right herself.

Every few nights she called Larry in California and asked him to please, please, just come back for the birth. He kept telling her, "Amy wouldn't like it."

Amy was the woman who had stolen Larry from her.

At her core Ellen was resilient and practical—no crisis could override that—so one day she took the bus down to the Health Unit and signed up for prenatal classes. Tuesday evenings for four weeks, babysitting provided. In the second class they practiced breathing exercises on mats. Ellen had to pair up with the instructor, which caused the pity level in the room to soar. Afterward a ringletty woman named Georgia, who was so petite and muscular her pregnancy barely showed, intercepted Ellen and asked if she wanted to go for coffee sometime.

"Oh, thank you!" Ellen gasped.

When they met later in the week, Georgia brought along Celine, the glamorous one who all through the class ostentatiously stroked her belly like she was accompanying them on the harp. She was much taller, massively pregnant, but only from the front and side. From the back, you couldn't tell. (Ellen just looked fat under all her loose garments so no-one offered her a seat on the bus.) By chance Georgia had run into Celine at the Royal Centre Mall, recognized her from the class and invited her along. None of them really knew each other.

Georgia, who seemed tactful and shy, might never have asked, but Celine did, the second their coffee mugs were set in front of them. There was a boldness to Celine, a right-to-knowness that, combined with her overall perfection—clothes, hair, skin—would have smacked of bourgeois entitlement on Cordova Island.

"So?" Celine asked Ellen. "Are you doing this on your own?"

"Apparently," Ellen said.

"What does that mean?"

The interrogation obviously pained Georgia, who had invited this stranger along. She stared into her mug, then shot Ellen a life-line kind of look. Except Ellen didn't take it. Bobbing far out beyond her pride, she wanted, needed, Celine's sympathy more.

"I *was* married. Until about a month ago."

"That's brave," Celine said, taking in Mimi too, squeezed onto what little remained of Ellen's lap, sucking on the crayons the waitress had brought. "I'm not sure I'd leave Richard in my condition. Not that I have reason to."

"It wasn't my idea," Ellen said.

18

"He left *you?*" Celine said and both women, instinctively and together, reached for Ellen. "What a *bastard!*"

Ellen wished Larry could hear how she limped to his defence. "He had his reasons, I guess." Then she started weeping. One reason was that she'd slipped up, too, but she didn't volunteer this fact. She let them comfort her, Georgia squeezing her hand, Celine beside her hugging hard. This was the sisterhood they had celebrated in the Cordova Island Hall once a month when the Women's Empowerment Group met, but which had proved to be a lie. Who would have thought she'd find it here, in a yuppie café on Lonsdale Avenue?

It was Celine who answered Ellen's call when her labour started, who took Mimi to Georgia's and coached Ellen all day, rubbing the small of her back, timing contractions, reading out from her notebook the pertinent passages they had covered in class. Who drove Ellen to the hospital six hours later and remained steadfastly with her in the delivery-room while Ellen, squatting, screamed out her agony. "I hate your fucking guts, Larry Silver! I hate you so much!"

For here was another lie: contrary to what they'd learned in prenatal class, the crowning of the baby's head is not necessarily a moment of pure joy. Ellen was, in fact, at her lowest then, the most Biblically wretched creature that had ever crawled the clodded surface of the earth. No-one could feel more abandoned, more utterly abject, than she, Ellen Silver, in her final push.

Two thousand kilometres away the father of the child ripping mercilessly through her body was probably screwing his tarty actress girlfriend *right that minute*. What could be worse than that?

Something. What happened to Celine was worse.

"Are you on crack?" Tony, her hairdresser, asked in 2008, the week before Ellen left on her trip to France with Celine. "*That* Celine? The quack? The one you complain about *every time* you come here?"

"Every time?" Ellen asked, surprised and a little ashamed she could be so consistently disloyal. She was relieved when Tony moved on to the subject at hand, Ellen's roots, how the grey was already showing again so how about something *dramatique?* "I could do something to you today that I guarantee will draw those horny Frenchmen to you like, like—They will *oo-la-la!* They will fall on those shit-covered French sidewalks trying to get a glimpse up your skort." (Ellen had brought her new skort in a bag to show Tony.) "They will curse that skort. *Merde, merde, merde*, they will say. I thought it was a skirt, but I can't see *anything!*"

"Skirt plus shorts. Skort," Ellen said again.

"It will put them into a frenzy, the skort together with what I could do to your hair, if only you'd let me. If only you would *laissez faire* your hair the way you have your life."

"Don't fuck up my hair, Tony."

"You take chances, Ellen. You'll probably screw 50 horny Frenchmen over there. Or you could. If you would let me do this one little thing."

"It's tempting," Ellen had said.

Now here she was! In France! In France, writing a postcard to Tony so he would get it before her next appointment. Until they adjusted to the time change, she and Celine were renting a 600 year-old house in a tiny village in the Luberon mountains. Celine, a practicing herbalist, was all messed up. She'd locked herself in her room. But Ellen had been liberal with the Zoplicone, even on the plane. (If it went down, she preferred to sleep through it.)

Ellen, in France, with her *café au lait* and chocolate *croissant* that she had ordered herself using actual French words, sitting in a village square waiting for a horny Frenchman she might claim in the postcard to have screwed to come along. Wild iris crowded the base of the fountain, *à la* Van Gogh. Chocolate bittersweet on her tongue. Then the bells in the eleventh-century church began to ring.

Oh my God, thought Ellen, clutching her head. *Sonnez les matines! Ding dang dong!*

It was almost too much, too beautiful.

She wrote on the card to Tony, *Who needs a man?*

Her relationship with Celine was complicated, more complicated than with Georgia, who had also expressed trepidation when Ellen told her about the hiking trip. Ellen and Celine had a long history together yet this history, full of tribulations for them both, as well as minor triumphs, did absolutely nothing to change Celine's attitude toward Ellen. Celine was (Ellen thought) frozen in the big-sister role she had taken on when they first met, a role that Ellen, who already had an older sister, frequently resented. All those years ago Ellen had been lost and desperate and she would never forget Celine's kindness to her, which was probably why they were still friends. (She was not so disloyal after all!) She just didn't want to be treated like a woebegone child at the age of 46.

This wasn't Georgia's take on it. Georgia said, "You're exactly alike. That's the problem."

"What? I'm flaky and judgmental?"

"Not flaky," Georgia conceded, which shut Ellen up. Every cell in Georgia's body was powered by honesty and loving-kindness. She was entirely without ego or wiles. Georgia deserved a constellation.

The proprietor of the 600-year-old house had stocked it with tourist brochures. Discovering it was market day in a nearby village, Ellen left a note for Celine and drove off in the rental car along narrow winding roads, past tidily arranged vineyards and olive groves. Even on the curves dozens of lead-footed Provençals, heedless of the dividing line or death, overtook her. Of course they could die. They'd already been to heaven, which was an actual Provençal market, Ellen knew by the return trip. The hatch of the Clio was stuffed with proof—a waxy yellow chicken, black and green tapenade, four kinds of chèvre. Baguettes. A pink, frilled, bridal bouquet of a lettuce. Two bottles of Chateauneuf-du-Pape. She would have bought more, but they were leaving in two days and Ellen would have to carry it all on her back.

That evening, with still no sign of Celine, Ellen set to cooking in the three-year-old kitchen in the 600-year-old house, happily into the wine, so happy, which was the purpose of the trip, Celine had claimed. To cheer Ellen up. She sang aloud to herself, rubbing the powdery fleur de sel into the puckered skin of the bird.

Until Celine shouted from her bedroom down the hall. "Can you be a little quieter in there, Ellen, for Christ's sake?"

Two days later Ellen was packed and ready and waiting for Celine. Waiting for Celine to finish her yoga routine, then waiting while Celine reorganized her backpack so the heavier things would be on the bottom. There were no heavy things in Ellen's backpack. It was practically weightless with newly purchased, feather-light, scrunchable travel clothes including a wrinkle-free peony of a little green dress that Ellen adored.

But for the first day of their hike she had put on the skort. She turned a circle for Celine. "What do you think?"

"Slimming," Celine said.

The remark deformed in Ellen's ear. She'd already lost ten pounds, but she was still too fat. Celine was too thin. Ellen suspected fasting and (shudder) herbal colonics zealously self-administered.

Finally, finally, Celine was ready. Bidding *adieu* to the hilltop village, they drove off to return the rental car in a town 40 minutes away, Celine at the wheel since she'd been to the area several times and knew the roads. On the way, she pointed out various landmarks. "See that chateau? It belonged to the Marquis de Sade." "That crossroads? That's the exact spot where Beckett got the idea for *Waiting For Godot*. Later in the week we'll come to the town where Camus died. We can picnic on his grave."

"Why didn't you tell me this before?" Ellen complained. She hadn't even considered *Justine* or *Molloy* or *L'étranger*. She'd brought Colette.

The rental car office was closed, not just for those two-hour French lunches. According the hand-written message Celine read on the door, it was shut for the whole long weekend.

"Is it the weekend?" Ellen asked.

"This is outrageous." Celine stormed over to the Clio, snatched the Europcar contract from the glove compartment. "It says we return it here. Today. Saturday, May 24th."

They found a pay phone a block away outside the train station. Celine bought a phone card then called in her complaint in French, not as fluently as she had let on. Ellen didn't think Celine sounded angry enough stammering like that so she muscled her aside.

"Do you speak English?"

The woman did, about as well as Celine spoke French, giving

Ellen the upper hand. Yet this lackey did not crumple the way her North American counterpart would when blasted with consumer discontent. She didn't even apologize, merely explained in charming accents that they should drive to the TGV station in Avignon where one of their offices was open. The two friends stomped back to the car, arms linked, for there is nothing more unifying than a common grievance, except maybe love.

After the two-hour wait in Avignon for the 40-minute train trip back to the same town they'd failed to return the car in, then a costly 30-minute cab ride, they arrived at the trailhead. It was in another hilltop village, this one partially abandoned, long-weekend tourists elbow-to-elbow among the ruined castle and the tiny ruined houses and the restored sixteenth-century church. The reinhabited part was full of shops. Ellen wanted to see the pottery before they left. By then it was 4:30 in the afternoon.

Before this trip, Ellen had not known that all of France was netted with walking trails. Celine showed her a red and white blaze on a wall, consulted the map, pointed straight ahead. Despite Ellen's apprehension about the late start, she tightened the straps of her pack (which was not, in fact, weightless, but fairly heavy by then), and followed Celine along what was at first a cobbled medieval road, then an ascending footpath. They'd already talked themselves out on the train, venting their mutual anger; no particular emotion replaced it for some time. Up they walked, up through a forest ringing electrically with cicadas. At their feet were wildflowers that Ellen cultivated in her own garden at home—candelabra primula, candy tuft, Lenten rose, muscari, euphorbia, daffodil—all in miniature. Even the trees seemed stunted. The insects, on the other hand, were gargantuan. A bee the size of her thumb bonked her on the temple. It felt like a stoning's introductory blow.

On the treeless crest, a wind reared up and almost blew them over. They bent into it, scrambling over the rocks, moving slowly, hair whipping around their heads. Below was the town where they had a reservation for the night, a manageable distance away, not that far, ten kilometres by the map. It would be easy now that they were going down, but down by the most up and down route possible, it turned out. Sometimes they missed the trail markings and had to backtrack. Or they stopped to consult the map, then argued about which way to go. If they took Celine's suggestion and met up with a bold red X on a rock, she wouldn't admit fault. She'd say, "Oh, not this way, I guess," despite how she had insisted they take that turn. If Ellen was wrong, though, Ellen would say sorry.

Meanwhile, Ellen was in pain. Feet, knees, back. "You've done this hike?" she asked.

Celine had not. "I told you that, Ellen."

She had only admired these mountains from a safe distance. Compared to *their* mountains, these were barely foothills, another French miniature, she had told Ellen, which was technically true, but ignored the fact of the very challenging terrain.

Dusk fell around eight and Ellen, who had been wordlessly trudging behind Celine, began to grumble again about the outrage perpetrated on them by Europcar. This was when Celine let slip a shocking fact: the office had been open.

"It's too bad we didn't get there before noon."

"What?" Ellen roared. "I was ready to go by nine! We could easily have gotten there if you hadn't taken two hours to pack your stuff!"

"There you go again, Ellen. Don't. Don't start with this blaming stuff."

"Why shouldn't I? It's your fault."

"Am I blaming you?"

"For what?"

"For dawdling in every one of those shops even though they all sell the same Provençal crap. We could have been on the trail an hour earlier."

"So you are blaming me."

"I'm saying you bear some responsibility, too. I choose not to blame. Blaming is toxic."

This was *exactly* Ellen's complaint to Tony: Celine's passive aggressive tendencies. "You blamed Europcar!" she shrilled.

She itched, just itched, to kick the skinny Lululemoned ass she'd been forced to look at for the last four hours, the ass she ended up looking at for two more, or rather, barely made out in the dark as they stumbled into the town and found the guest house and roused the owner who, as he showed them their room, confessed that he'd lost hope they would show up.

"*J'ai perdu l'espoir.*"

Even Ellen understood that.

Ellen didn't kick Celine's skinny ass. She couldn't because Celine's baby had died all those years ago when Ellen's and Georgia's babies had been born healthy and lusting for life. It had squirmed in its incubator for two days, and then it died. It had no brain.

When Ellen woke the next morning after eight hours of undrugged sleep, she remembered that terrible time, Celine's milk coming in for nothing, her tranced shuffling around her house of grief, belly still huge with the dead space the baby had left in her life. And Ellen's heart went out to Celine snoring lightly in the adjacent twin bed. Celine, her dear friend whom she loved. Celine, who was not half so annoying when unconscious.

At breakfast, Ellen asked, "How far today?"

Celine showed her the map. Twenty-five kilometres. At least they would be on the trail in good time. They agreed to rest more frequently, to eat more, to be kinder to each other.

"I'm sorry I lost it yesterday," Ellen said.

Celine said, "Oh, Ellen. Never mind."

Stiff from the day before, they hobbled back through the stone town, stopping for the baguettes they stuffed arrow-like in the quiver of their packs. Celine, a vegetarian, waited outside the *boucherie* while Ellen bought herself a donkey sausage.

Every muscle screamed. The tender spots on Ellen's feet pulsated, despite the moleskin. Two hours of slow, silent climbing back up the rock-studded, thyme-scrubbed side of the mountain they had wrecked their knees coming down the night before. Gradually, Ellen felt herself detach. It was as if she was already out of this situation telling someone about it later. Who? Georgia?

Tony. *En garding* in the mirror with the scissors, rolling his eyes. She was telling tell him about the trip, how Celine hadn't come out of her room the first two days, how bossy she'd been with the map.

"A country of what? *Sixty million?* And you couldn't find *one single* horny Frenchman to screw you?"

25

They rested on some boulders next to the trail. While Celine drank her boiled water, Ellen, taking an advance on lunch, joked about Tony's hopes for her. Celine's lips tightened.

"Don't be such a prude," Ellen said, poking her with the gnawed-on baguette.

"I'm just not into those types of relationships. You know that Ellen. I would find it demeaning."

Celine got off the rock she was sitting on, swung her pack onto her back. She was visibly shorter with it on, three inches at least. "You charge at men," she said.

"I used to," Ellen said. "I haven't for some time."

This was less because she'd stopped waving the red cape of her need than because no-one came near enough to see it.

"They don't respect you and you don't respect yourself."

"Okay, okay," Ellen said, holding out her hand. Celine helped her up, Ellen groaning loudly, not just for effect.

"Let's sing," Ellen said, trying for a lighter tone. "Let's make a joyful noise."

They didn't know the same songs, so they took turns. Celine's repertoire was meagre, Ellen's vast—all the jazz standards her mother used to sing, the hippy songs from Cordova Island. (*We Shall Overcome* seemed particularly *apropos*.) Soon Ellen was doing all the singing and, when she realized it, she stopped, thinking that maybe she was annoying Celine. Maybe Celine was at that moment far in the future complaining to Georgia about how Ellen wouldn't stop singing on the trail. How she actually wasn't that great a singer. Ellen couldn't tell what Celine was thinking since her back was continually to Ellen as she set their bovine pace.

"Moo," Ellen said.

Celine looked over her shoulder. "What's that supposed to mean?"

"Nothing. I was just mooing."

Never had putting one foot in front of the other seemed so gruelling! "Celine? My feet? My metatarsals? They're aching like you would not believe. I don't think I've ever experienced pain like this. Childbirth was nothing."

And her shoulders—so tight. It wasn't hot, the temperature was, in fact, perfect —everything so fucking perfect!—yet she

26

poured out sweat.

After lunch, when precious energy diverted toward digestion, when jet lag struck again (it had not been vanquished after all, only temporarily staved off), Ellen's default switch tripped to the Brood About Larry position. Her bra was saturated. There were wet patches, like when she nursed her babies.

Larry's abandoned babies.

"I get so angry!" Ellen said, slogging on, wishing vainly for Celine to say the right thing.

"Issues, Ellen," Celine sighed.

"I know I have issues. I'm trying. Don't you ever think of Richard?"

Ahead of her Celine stiffened, reclaiming her three lost inches. "No."

Ellen herself hadn't thought of Richard in years, could barely picture the effete-looking man of the pre-natal classes, the stunned one from the funeral. Before the baby, Celine had been a meat-eating, middle class suburban wife with a government job. Richard hadn't made it into the After frame of Celine's Before-and-After life. Larry, though, was still very much in Ellen's because of their daughters. But also because, after all they had been through, they were simply connected, for better or for worse.

They were back in the woods, which seemed eerily quiet for a holiday weekend. They'd encountered no-one on the trail. When eventually they came to a gravel road, Ellen looked at Celine. Hair sticking to her pale face, Celine was obviously suffering as much as Ellen, maybe more, just not complaining about it. She pointed her chin up the road. Ellen deferred. Moments later, they saw the rude red X on a tree trunk, turned and headed the other way.

"Oh, great," Ellen said, pointing at another X.

"It must be here," said Celine, walking straight into the trees on the other side of the road. Ellen had no opinion now, was simply stumbling along behind Celine. Celine could lead her off a cliff if she wanted.

The trees were deciduous. Ellen marked each syllable with a step. Dee-sid-you-us. She sensed them, these trees, their straight grey trunks so evenly spaced in her peripheral vision. You-us.

Dee-sid. And something flipped. She and Celine were standing still and the trees were advancing on them, surrounding them. But trees didn't have feet. (Oh, not to have feet!) She turned her head and saw this was silly, the trees weren't moving. Instead, someone was watching them and had been for a long time.

Not the trees, *from* them.

But no-one was there. All Ellen saw was ashen bark, the bright green coinage of leaves. How old were they, these French trees? Young. Someone must have planted them after the war. Which war? They'd had so many. Also this terrible massacre of a Protestant sect a few centuries ago. Ellen had read about it in the guidebook.

She came to enough to ask if Celine had actually seen a marker. "Just back there," Celine told her and Ellen, believing her, plodded on because if she stopped she would never start again.

"I haven't," she said after a while. "I haven't seen any marker for a long long time."

It was dead people. Centuries of them. The dead were watching them from the trees. Just then Celine sank down on the path, as if she'd had the same realization, and the weight of her pack tipped her onto her side and held her there. Out of her rose a wrenching, leaf-stirring sob.

Ellen looked down at her. "I shouldn't have mentioned Richard."

"Shush!"

"I'm sorry, Celine."

Ellen undid her own pack and let it thud to the ground. The relief was exquisite, but short-lived. When she knelt to unfasten Celine's buckles and liberate her, a burning pain ripped up her thighs.

Celine sobbed. "I thought you could use this trip, Ellen. That's what I thought."

Ellen's father had killed himself. (Was he here too? Ellen looked around.) He'd drowned himself last December while visiting Ellen. He seemed to have come specifically to do it and Ellen didn't know why. It still hurt, and it hurt to be reminded of it. Celine, more than anyone, understood this. It was Celine's reason for inviting Ellen to France.

At that moment Ellen simply gave up. She curled in a ball on the forest floor among the tiny wildflowers and the super-sized bugs, and closed her eyes. She didn't give a flying fuck what happened next.

Which was they both fell asleep. When they woke, they were cold and stiff nearly to the point of paralysis, and utterly alone.

Somehow they struggled to their feet. Dried leaves and dirt decorated their hair. Celine's face was streaked with mud. Ellen lifted Celine's pack for her to put on; Celine lifted Ellen's. Equally burdened, they limped back to the road where they turned in unison and carried on downhill, right past the X, completely in sync, as if they never, ever disagreed on anything.

"We're too old for this," Ellen told Celine from her twin bed that night, when it all seemed funny. "I mean, we're middle aged. Didn't that occur to you?"

Celine said, "Speak for yourself."

"We might have died out there. Now I've bonded with that boy. He saved our lives. I'm in love with him."

"His name is Oog," Celine said.

"What?"

"That's what he said."

"That's unfortunate."

Celine rolled over so her back was to Ellen. She giggled.

"What?" Ellen asked.

"I'm surprised you aren't screwing him right now."

"I would! *He* wouldn't. I'm too old."

Ten minutes down the road they had come to a riding stable. "I'm stealing a horse," Ellen had said, but when they staggered into the barn a young man was there brushing the animals. Celine asked in French for a phone to call a cab. Despite her exhaustion, Ellen got the gist of what he told Celine in reply, that he was actually a prince, not a lowly, well-built stable boy, that he had been waiting a hundred years for them to stumble in and break the cruel spell that had been cast on him.

Celine turned to Ellen, tears shining in her eyes. "He's going to drive us!"

His van was white, further proof of his enchantment. Celine immediately claimed the passenger seat, because she spoke

French. Ellen hoped this didn't mean that she got to marry him. No, Ellen did because she was relegated to the horsy smelling back of the van that had no seats, just a foam mattress. Ellen was Cinderella. The prince threw in their packs, and his, and a rolled up sleeping bag. He offered his hand and Ellen climbed in.

With just one touch, her pain vanished.

Up front, Celine explained their predicament. "Ellen? He says he can drop us off in Loumarin, or we can go where he's going. Another town a little further. He has a friend there who runs a winery with a campground and a *gîte*. A hostel. He says there's even a pool."

Ellen said, "I go wherever he goes."

The next morning Ellen woke alone in the cramped room at the top of the stairs. Two twin beds separated by a night table. A wardrobe for their things. Stiff, battered, she limped to the window. Celine was down in the vineyard, saluting the Provençal sun, her purple yoga mat unrolled between the vines.

A twenty-minute walk in sandals brought Ellen to the large stone reservoir surrounded by plane trees in the centre of town. Café tables clustered on one side. Here she sat for the rest of the morning in perfect contentment with her *café au lait* and *croissant*, writing a postcard to each of her grown daughters, notifying them that they had very nearly been left motherless. Then she poked around the town buying delicacies for lunch.

On the way back to the *gîte* she spotted the white van of their saviour, Oog, in the adjacent campground. The stone house, bearded with ivy between bright blue shutters, was divided, one side the elderly proprietors' residence, the other the *gîte*. Despite the campground being full, Ellen and Celine were the only guests. It was normally only open in summer, Celine had translated the night before. They had made an exception for Celine and Ellen since they had come with Oog.

Now a truck about the size of a moving van was backed against the barn-like building that stood at a right angle to the house. Celine and the old woman were sitting together at one of the picnic tables under the trees. "They're bottling the wine," Celine told Ellen when she walked up. "And his name is

Hugues. *Hugh.* It's pronounced differently in French."

"I'll say."

The old woman's filamentous hair suggested illness; it barely concealed her pink scalp. She smiled at Ellen. *"Bonjour,"* Ellen said, *"Comment allez-vous?"* and this malpronounced greeting unleashed a long gravelly reply, which Celine had to translate.

"She's asking how you slept."

"Très bon." Ellen sat down with her provisions at her feet, but gave up on the conversation. She was still deeply tired and the French floated around her in the scented air with the strange insects and the masculine voices in the barn and the machinery sounds. Now and then she understood something Celine said to the old woman. *Divorcée.* The old woman gestured to the barn, got up and went into the house.

"She's making their lunch," Celine said.

Ellen went into their side of the house to do the same, to the *gîte* kitchen, stashing the bottle of rosé in the freezer while she assembled a tray. She brought it back out to Celine. "I am going to be so fat when this is over."

"Don't eat so much," Celine said.

"What would be the point then?"

Ellen shook the water off a lettuce leaf, dipped it directly into a saucer of walnut oil, salted it. Some of the oil ran down her chin and christened the front of her little green dress. She opened the wine. Celine wouldn't drink in the daytime. She would only eat the lettuce and a bit of baguette and chèvre.

Though Ellen's back was to the barn, she could tell from Celine's face when the men came out. "You're blushing," she said.

Hugues walked right over in his undershirt and pirate bandana, bringing the son of the old couple, who looked in his early forties. He had fine brown hair, rolled sleeves and glasses with thick frames. Hugues nodded to Celine and said, "Hélène," by way of introducing her. Ellen he called Celine.

"Actually, *I'm* Ellen," said Ellen, shaking the hand the son extended to her.

"Jean-François," he said. "John-Frank."

"Ah," said Ellen, "Someone I can talk to."

"Not today, I regret. We are embottling the wine."

Hugues and Jean-François entered the house while the other

31

workers washed at an outside tap then gathered at a picnic table across the yard. The food came out in several trips, carried by the old couple and Hugues and Jean-François—an armload of baguette, two casserole dishes, cheeses, three bottles of wine. The old man, very Cezanne in his straw hat, waved to them. Now and then Ellen glanced over her shoulder to admire the unselfconscious way the men ate, bowed low over their plates, tearing at the bread, swallowing the wine like water.

"We're quite a bit ahead of schedule now," Celine said. "Do you want to stay here a few days and rest up?"

"Do you?" Ellen asked.

Tuesday after the long weekend the campground emptied out— no more screeching children, no radios playing American rap. The bottling was finished and the enchanting Hugues drove off in his white van, stirring up clouds of dust and yearning. The next few mornings glided into routine: Celine drank her herbal tinctures, yogaed, swam in the pool, while Ellen walked to town for *petite dejeuner* and postcard writing and a few chapters of *Chéri* by the reservoir. In the afternoon, they hiked with daypacks. Afterward the old man, who had been born in the area and was something of a naturalist, would look at the pictures on Ellen's camera and name all the bugs and flowers in French.

They came across the bizarrest sight on Thursday. A trail of caterpillars almost two metres long, each holding onto the caterpillar in front. This prompted a long incomprehensible story from Mr. Cezanne. (They were calling him this to his face now and he liked it.) He got Celine and Ellen up, Celine's hands on his waist, Ellen's on Celine's, and they marched around the yard, laughing.

"We're getting along better here," Celine told Ellen when they were tucked into their twin beds that night.

"That's because you're not being such a bitch," Ellen said and Celine actually smiled. Neither mentioned getting back on the trail.

The follow morning a car pulled alongside Ellen as she was walking to town. "*Âllo!* Celine!"

"John-Frank," said Ellen, recognizing the emphatic glasses more than the rather vague driver. "I'm Ellen."

"Hélène! Sorry!" he called across the empty passenger seat. "You see, in French they are confusable names. *Say-leen. Ay-len.*"

About as similar as *Hyoo* and *Oog* were different, Ellen thought. She told Jean-François, "We don't even look alike."

Jean-François drew back in surprise. "You do. Let me drive you, Hélène."

"I'm supposed to be on a walking holiday. Thanks though."

"Celine isn't walking," Jean-François said, still matching her pace in the Audi. "I saw her in the vineyard. Exercising."

"She's like that," Ellen said. "Where did you learn English?"

"Canada."

"Really? Where?"

Actually, he'd learned it in university but spent six months in Canada last year helping friends set up a winery. "You probably don't know this place. Kelowna."

"Of course I do. I'm from British Columbia."

"No!"

Then a funny thing happened. In his amazement Jean-François let go of the wheel. There was no verge. Ellen was on the very edge of the road next to some prickly sort of hedge. As the car veered toward her, she instinctively put out her hand, as if she could actually stop several thousand pounds of machine from running into her. And when that didn't work, she smacked the hood hard.

Jean-François braked just in time. "I wonder. No." He shook his head.

Ellen bent to look in the window. "What?"

"If you know my friends. Mireille and Réné Vardon? No, see? I always expect too much. Still, it's amazing you ended up here, don't you think?"

Ellen resumed walking, still accompanied by Jean-François. No-one honked. She hadn't heard a single horn in France. Traffic swerved around the crawling Audi and eventually Ellen and her escort reached the reservoir where Jean-François parked the car on the sidewalk and leapt out. At one of the café tables, he pulled out a chair for her and hurried inside, returning momentarily with two espressos.

Ellen felt a tiny bit annoyed. Because this life would not last forever and she wanted it just so for as long as possible, the ritual of her *croissant* and bowl of coffee. She wanted to order it herself, to say out loud what were practically the only French words she knew. But then she thought, why not? Jean-François wasn't good-looking, but he wasn't bad-looking either, especially now that Hugues was gone. He had a sexy, hyphenated name and a sexy accent, particularly the way he said "the Okanagan."

Ellen had been to Kelowna once and thought it was a dump.

"What's a dump?" Jean-François asked.

"You probably don't have them here," Ellen said.

He picked *Chéri* off the table and studied it. "How long are you staying?"

"Actually," Ellen said. "I might never go back."

"That would be pleasant," Jean-François said, still looking at the book.

A fluttering started inside Ellen that was very pleasant in itself, like a cloud of butterflies inhaled. She looked at Jean-François to see if he meant what she thought he meant. And, smiling, he pointed to the plain orange and beige cover of the book with its jaunty little penguin. "*Chéri*. Darling."

Flutter, flutter.

Jean-François didn't live with his old parents, but in an apartment in town. He went back and forth all day. When Ellen said she was picking up groceries, he offered to meet her back at the car in an hour. "I'll take your food for you. So you can have your walk."

It seemed only right to ask him to dinner.

On their hike that afternoon, Ellen and Celine passed a vineyard where a tractor was spewing a greenish powder over the rows of vines. The breeze shifted and the cloud about-faced and headed for the path Celine and Ellen were walking on. Celine clapped a hand over her mouth and nose and ran.

When Celine told Jean-François about it at dinner, he grew indignant. They did not apply pesticides or anti-fungals to their vines. As soon as he said this, Celine took a bolder sip of the wine he'd brought, pronounced it delicious, then went on to have two full glasses—about half what Ellen had been drinking every night. Celine possessed an almost translucent, unlined complexion that Ellen thought of as pallid when she felt

34

uncharitable. The wine made this rosier Celine laugh freely, with her head back so her hair, blonde camouflaging the grey, brushed her narrow shoulder blades. But every time Ellen glanced across the table to see the effect Celine was having on Jean-François, he smiled at Ellen.

He had two children who lived up in Lyon with their mother. He turned to Ellen. "You are divorced, too."

"Who told you that?" Ellen asked.

"My mother," he said.

Ellen could have said that there were three people sitting at the long table whose marriages had failed, or who had failed their marriages, though afterward she was glad she hadn't because it had been a perfect evening. Jean-François didn't seem to want it to end. Ellen served lamb, massaged, kneaded and spanked until the thyme she'd gathered on the trail had penetrated the flesh. Jean-François praised it and, while Celine only ate the lentils and the salad, she told Jean-François that Ellen was spoiling her with her cooking. And it seemed to Ellen that whenever she left the common-room and went to the kitchen for another course, she could feel Jean-François's eyes, darkly framed by the glasses, following her. She was wearing the green dress.

He looked at his watch, heaved a Gallic shrug, rose. Celine and Ellen walked him out to his Audi where he kissed them each three times—left cheek, right cheek, left cheek. To Ellen he said, very tenderly, "*Bonne nuit, Celine.*" And to Celine, "*Bonne nuit, Hélène.*"

Both women burst out laughing.

Going up to their room, Ellen stumbled. She would have screwed Jean-François if Celine hadn't been there. If Celine had gone to bed instead of yawning on the floor of the common-room with her long legs twisted into the lotus position. Why hadn't she? Celine didn't want to screw him. She would have found it demeaning.

Ellen shook a Zoplicone out of the bottle, squinted at its turquoiseness.

"Are you sure you want to take that, Ellen? After all you drank? I can prepare you a remedy that will work just was well."

Surprise, surprise, she was angry in the morning. Angry and hung over. Celine was still in bed, sleeping holistically after her temperate evening, until Ellen asked, loudly, "Why do you have to tell everyone I'm divorced?"

Celine's eyes flew open.

"It makes me feel like a failure," Ellen said.

Celine sighed. "You're not a failure, Ellen. Larry's a failure."

"Larry's a failure? Larry is the most successful person you know." She clutched her headache. Why did she defend him all the time?

"Ellen? I've said it before. Here I go again. Larry is a jerk. He screwed everyone. Forget about him."

"Did he screw you?" Ellen asked.

"I wouldn't let Larry near me."

"Then what do you know about it?"

"You told me!" Celine said, throwing back the covers and springing up. "You've told me so many times!" She turned her bony back to Ellen, stripped off her pyjama top, struggled into her bra.

"You seem angry," Ellen said.

"Oh, shut up."

"You are. You're angry. So did you sleep with Larry or not?"

Celine drove one leg, then the other, into tiny cotton panties. She yanked them over her enviably skinny ass.

"Why aren't you answering me? Yes, or no?"

Celine grabbed her clothes and her yoga mat and walked out. Definitely angry.

As soon as Ellen got to town, she bought a postcard for Georgia. At the café, she wrote: *Sitting beside a reservoir. About to fling myself in.* Like her father had. *Then this holiday will be over!*

She felt like it. She really did.

Instead, she opened Colette, dragged her eyes down the page. It didn't make sense. Léa loses her young lover, her darling Chéri, to her rival's daughter. Now she looks in the mirror and sees *an old woman, out of breath…what she could have in common with that crazy creature?*

What crazy creature? Ellen turned the page. *The End?*

She gathered up her things and went inside to pay. They

would never come out. You could die at your table, your face on the plate, flies swarming above you, and they wouldn't come out.

In the café bathroom, she combed her hair, which she had apparently neglected to do before leaving the *gîte*. She picked the grains of sleep out of her eyes.

The walk back helped. Twice, she dropped Colette because she had to keep hoisting her stretched-out skort. Each time she bent over to pick the book off the dusty side of the road, her mood relaxed its hold a little. By the time she reached the campground, it was dawning on her that she had behaved badly.

Surprise, surprise.

Celine was in the pool. It was unheated, too cold for Ellen, she had discovered the first day when she dipped her hand in. Celine, though, was made of stiffer stuff and there stood Jean-François, watching Celine ply the waters. Ellen watched him watching her friend's long lithe body glide the blue length of the pool, his glasses trained on her, magnifying her, bringing her closer. Who could blame him? Celine looked 30 underwater.

Jean-François glanced up and, seeing Ellen, hurried over. "There was a dead mouse in the pool this morning. I didn't have time to get it out. I came to tell her. But maybe I shouldn't now. What she doesn't know? *Ça ne la blessera pas.*"

He followed Ellen away from the pool. "What's wrong?"

"Nothing."

"You are crying."

She blinked through the sudden tears. She was ashamed of how she had goaded Celine that morning—Celine who was like a sister to her. "It's nothing. It's stupid." Her skirt was hanging low on her hips. She yanked it up and Colette fell to the ground again. And Ellen remembered the last line of the book and her own harried face in the café mirror, uglier for never, ever being in the wrong.

"I finished my book," she told Jean-François as she bent to pick it up. "I didn't bring another."

"We have books!" Jean-François guided her by the elbow toward the *gîte*. "English books. People leave them."

In the common-room where they had eaten the night before,

he pulled something off the shelf. Dean Koontz. He squeezed her shoulders, ran his hands up and down her bare arms as she clasped both books to her chest. When he kissed her, it was full on the lips, not alternate cheeks, and for a long time. He tangoed her against the bookshelf and lapped inside her mouth. And Ellen kissed him back like she had nothing to lose, which was true. Her whole face felt covered in slobber by the time they separated.

Jean-François searched his pocket and came up with a scrap, a receipt it looked like. "Write your email address. Here." There was a jar on the shelf. "Here is a pen."

When she had written her address, he took the receipt. Then he took her book, kissing her wrist as payment. "I am going to read this book about Colette."

"Actually, it's about Chéri," Ellen said.

"It will be good for my English. Now I have to go back to work. You're not leaving yet? Will I see you later?"

"I sure hope so," Ellen said.

Upstairs, the shower was running, meaning Celine had probably walked right past the open door of the common-room while the edge of the bookshelf was impressing itself upon the small of Ellen's back. Ellen lay on her bed. She could still feel it, the ridge digging into her spine, the fullness of two tongues in her mouth.

The shower turned off. A few minutes later, Celine came in. Seeing Ellen, she made a sound. Disgust maybe. Or hurt.

"I'm sorry," Ellen said.

"Oh, right," Celine said.

"I am."

Celine began to apply some kind of balm to her lips. When she finished, she asked, "Do you want to go or stay?"

"What do you want to do?" Ellen said.

"I don't care either way."

But Ellen could tell that she did.

"Let's go then," she said.

The last four days of the hike were on flatter terrain, much of it on roads. They felt almost merry, walking along, Ellen suffused with longing the whole way. She couldn't stop thinking about the kiss and that maybe Jean-François would write. How glad she was that they'd left before she screwed him. Because sometimes a kiss was enough. The bittersweetness of it. He had picked her. Picked her like a fruit.

In Ellen's experience, the promise of love was usually more pleasurable than its fulfilment.

She told Celine, "Thank you for bringing me here. I love it. I would come back in a second."

On the roadside, frequent casualties—*les papillons*, (another word she knew!), their wings a startling blue, or variations of orange and brown. Flutter, flutter. All along the way, she took pictures of the inch-high daffodils and the bizarre beetles they encountered on the trails. She used Celine's hand as a frame of reference.

Otherwise no-one would believe her.

Tony got her postcard.

"I *kissed* someone," she told him at her next appointment. "Doesn't that count? Against a bookcase. I almost slipped a disc. And Tony? It was a *French* kiss."

Tony said, *"Oo-la-la!"*

Two weeks after they got back, Celine phoned to say that Jean-François had emailed.

"I didn't realize you exchanged addresses," Ellen said, perhaps in a give-away tone, because Celine clammed up after that.

"What did he say?"

"Nothing. Just hello. Anyway, I should go."

"Thanks for telling me," Ellen said. She was already checking her own email. Nothing from Jean-François, just a long anxious message from her daughter Mimi in Toronto.

Georgia called fifteen minutes later. Ellen was still at her desk, rooted there in shock. "What happened on your trip that you didn't tell me about, Ellen?"

Ellen had wanted to savour Jean-François a little longer, to keep him a secret, to see what might happen if she didn't charge at a man for a change. But it had never been secret. Celine was in on it, though she hadn't mentioned, or even hinted at, seeing Ellen and Jean-François kiss.

"Celine just phoned me," Georgia said. "She's got a thing going with some guy there."

Obviously, Jean-François had kissed Celine, too, in between ogling her in the pool. He had wooed Ellen in town, then driven back to the *gîte* to woo Celine. That kiss, which Ellen had cherished as a rarity, a curiosity, a delicate and precious wonder, it meant nothing.

"He was nothing," she told Georgia. "Just French. It made him seem more attractive than he really was. And you know what? I'm never travelling with Celine again. She has to have her way with everything. Where we stayed, where we ate. But she's never up front about it. You discuss it and, lo and behold, you're doing what she wants every time. She's the same here. All because of a dead baby."

There. She said it. And shuddered in triumph.

"Ellen," Georgia said.

"You know it's true. Even now, when I mention Mimi or Yolanda, she tenses up. How dare I remind her of her loss! Unless it's something bad. When Mimi had drug troubles? It was all Celine could do not to rub her hands together in glee."

"What happened to Celine was awful."

"And it was a long long time ago. Enough is enough. What was it called? What it died of?" Ellen, still at the computer, tried to type it in.

Mr. Google said: *Did you mean anencephalathy?*

"And Ellen?" Georgia said. "I got your postcard. What did you mean?"

A picture of an anencephalatic baby popped up on the screen, a little saucer-eyed alien, its head flattened just above the eyebrows, staring out at Ellen. Ellen stared back, unable to close the window or turn away. Grotesque, piteous, the creature looked right into her empty place. And Ellen shuddered again to think what it saw there. Yet the body was normal and human. No, look. Oh, Christ! The poor little thing had no fingers. No fingers on its tiny little hands.

She pressed her forehead to the cold desk. "Georgia. I'm hanging up. I can't talk about this any more."

"Jean-François believes in destiny. Like I do," Celine told Ellen later that summer.

"Oh, puke," Ellen said. "You hardly know the guy."

"We email every day. Several times."

"You should be careful," Ellen said. "You can get cancer from too much screen time. Horrible tumours all over your face."

"You'll find someone, too, Ellen. As soon as you renounce your negativity. It really works. So will you come or will you stay home and pout?"

"I think I'll come and pout," Ellen said.

She goes to Celine's dinner party even though she doesn't like Celine's food. Once Celine served three different potato dishes in the same meal, another time fried tofu bologna. Anyway, Ellen is trying to keep off those eight pounds that she unexpectedly dropped on the trail in France, and the ten she lost after her father killed himself, so why not? She brings two bottles of Chateauneuf-du-Pape.

Jean-François leaps up from the couch when Ellen comes in the door, bestows the triple kiss—left cheek, right cheek, left cheek. Unfortunately, he looks better than she remembered, mostly because she's been downplaying him in her mind all day. The unflattering glasses, the beige hair. Dean Koontz! The hair got thinner and thinner until she could see his not-so-innocent scalp shining through, which only makes his hair seem thicker now. Also, his glasses are new, the frames smaller and rounder, she thinks. He looks so plaintive.

Georgia and her husband Gary were invited, too, so the conversation turns political. Luckily, Jean-François is a Green, which keeps the shouting to a bearable level. European politics—left, right, left—who can figure it out? Ellen sips her wine and smiles, pleased by how little she actually feels after her day-long snit. Every time her eyes and Jean-François's cross paths, she forces herself to blink.

Before dessert, she comes out of the bathroom. "Ah!"

Jean-François is there, lurking in the hall.

"Sorry," Ellen tells him. "You should have knocked."

"I was waiting," he explains. "Waiting to speak with you."

Ellen is a little drunk. In the bathroom, she was wondering if she stopped drinking now could she still drive home.

"I thought I was writing *you*," he says.

He means, *help me,* and glances back down the hall to the dining-room where Celine is dishing out rubbery squares of tofu cheesecake.

Jean-François leans into Ellen. She responds, leaning into him so they meet in the middle of this terrible gap of geography and misunderstanding. Then, instinctively, she puts out her hand. Drunkenly, with a strength she didn't even know she possessed, she smacks it flat against Jean-François's chest, pinning his eager heart beneath her palm.

This way, she holds him back.

Because, when Yolanda was born, Celine was the first to cradle her, even before Ellen. Celine, who kept sniffing the top of the baby's head, the dark, pasted down fluff. Celine was a week over-due then.

She told Ellen, "I can't wait. I just can't wait."

The Everpresent Hell of Other People

Marjorie Celona

At 4:52 PM, Harrison booked room 702 at the Estelle Hotel on Davidson Street, and Jean-Philippe booked the same room a mere five minutes later (they determined this via their confirmation emails), and Claude was already in the elevator, flanked by two red suitcases, the key to room 702 tucked in the palm of her hand. Harrison felt triumphant, believing the room to be the last in the city, and lucky: alone, in a beautiful hotel room overlooking the ocean, he would have an uninterrupted view of the storm. He had spent all morning on the phone, then all afternoon on the computer, searching for an available room. The city overflowed. Tens of thousands of people had come for the spectacle, and those who were residents were no better off in the backyards of their single-story homes, the best vantage point being at least five stories up, and facing west. At the last minute, office buildings rented their top floors, and students and low-income families camped out on air mattresses and yoga mats. Those more prosperous—Harrison—packed lightly and booked a night at the city's finest hotel.

Jean-Philippe entered the room an hour after Claude, who was inspecting the little bottles of lotion and didn't hear him over the bathroom fan. He sat on the bed and made a phone call to his mother—

"When the sun goes down, I'll call you, and I'll describe everything that I can see. It will be as if you are here with me."

—and when Claude opened the bathroom door and saw Jean-Philippe on the bed, she began to scream. It was at this moment that Harrison walked in.

A geomagnetic storm of this magnitude hadn't happened since

43

1859. What Harrison understood, to the best of his ability, was that a giant magnetic explosion—a "white light solar flare"—had occurred on the sun, and a huge cloud of charged particles was now hurtling toward Earth. The power would apparently go out (it did), as would telephone communication, even cellular phones (the last thing Jean-Philippe managed to convey to his mother was that two other people had somehow reserved *his* hotel room). GPS and satellite-to-ground communications would cease for an indeterminate amount of time. All planes would be grounded; ships docked. Everyone was to seek shelter, preferably where they could have an uninterrupted view of the sky—the government issued safety glasses, special sunscreen, and a pamphlet about the possibility of burns and blindness—and wait. Scientists could not say for certain how far the auroras would travel—the storm of 1859 could be seen as far south as Cuba—but a story quickly spread that the storm would be the most brilliant directly above the city in which Harrison lived. And, so, people came.

For $500, Harrison reserved room 702 at the Estelle Hotel. It was a "chalet-style" room, "chalet-style" meaning small. A double bed dwarfed by a white duvet and twelve white pillows took up most of the north-facing wall, with only a few inches separating it from a west-facing floor-to-ceiling window. The window looked out onto a small Juliet balcony, which was accessible by a sliding door. On the other side of the bed was a massive bronze statue of a faceless man, one arm outstretched, a rotary telephone resting in his palm. The television hung unceremoniously from a metal arm bolted into the wall, giving the whole thing the look of a luxurious hospital room. Red- and burgundy-striped wallpaper lined the walls and the floor was carpeted in blue velvet plush, so thick that every step left footprints. The bathroom had no shower. Harrison couldn't imagine what kind of guest would reserve this room and wondered immediately if it was for the staff, or something jerry-rigged for the occasion. His first thought upon entering the room was that he was a fool (a tall, blonde-haired woman in hysterics and a young man in a Laplander hat looking outraged were far too strange for him to process). He thought immediately of his wife and their argument that morning. She came from a small family—a mother and one brother—that Harrison had never felt comfortable around and secretly believed hated him deeply. She—his wife—wanted them all to hike to the top of Mount Yeoman, about a twenty-minute drive from the city, and watch the spectacle outside, with a picnic dinner and blankets. Harrison worried the drive would take hours, even though people were driving *into* the city and not out of it—he worried such a crowd would mutiny, cross the meridian, and advance toward the city in the wrong lane, throwing caution to the wind, as it were, in the face of such an event. He worried about being trapped in that car for hours. Her family had inside jokes, music they liked, stories they told, and it bored the hell out of him. He could not bear to be around it. And especially not during an event such as this. This was something he wanted to experience alone, without the influence of emotion—other people's emotions—without anyone needing anything from him. He wanted to think only of himself.

"Be alone then. Alone, alone, alone," were his wife's last words to him, and he said nothing in reply. He watched from their living-room window as she stuffed a blue cooler full of sandwiches into the trunk of the car, shoved blankets into the backseat, and pulled out her cell phone, presumably to tell her mother and brother that she was on her way.

Now here he was, in the doorway of the smallest hotel room in the world, and another couple—or so Harrison assumed—were busy hating each other.

"EEE!" Claude made a dolphin-like sound, and advanced toward Jean-Philippe with her arms outstretched, like a mummy come to life. She spun and came toward Harrison, still making the sound, and Jean-Philippe grabbed a pillow and threw it against the wall.

"Shut up!" he said. "Get out of my hotel room and shut up!"

Harrison didn't know of whom to be more frightened. Jean-Philippe was young—he looked about 23—and wore tight black jeans that tapered around his ankles, a black button-up shirt, and moccasins without socks. He was too lean and had a gigantic Adam's apple that protruded from his neck like a peach pit. He threw his Laplander hat onto the bed, ran his hand through his hair—greasy and brown, chin-length—and took three small breaths, in rapid-fire succession.

"My name is Jean-Philippe Rousseau, and this is my hotel room. Please leave immediately."

Claude dug into her purse and pulled out her room key. "It's my room. You are mistaken." The key instilled in her a new confidence, and she stood in the middle of the room, pointing it at Jean-Philippe's forehead. She looked to be in her forties, an olive-skinned woman with dark hair dyed blonde and tied back in a loose bun; blunt bangs. She wore a beige suit jacket, white blouse, and black leggings. She was barefoot. She held the key like a gun.

"You're both wrong." Here was Harrison, in his late thirties, in baggy blue jeans and a denim shirt, a duffel bag at his side, and wearing tan suede sneakers with white socks. He, too, held a room key. "Mine says, clearly, room 702."

"Then it's a mix-up." Claude pushed past him and padded barefoot toward the elevator, leaving Harrison with Jean-Philippe.

"Oh, for fuck sakes," Jean-Philippe said, and then they were all in the elevator together, headed toward the lobby.

When the doors opened, none of them moved. Jean-Philippe took a hesitant step forward and Harrison put his hand on his shoulder, pulling him back. It was a goddamn madhouse in that lobby. There must have been 200 people crammed around the concierge's desk, all wiggling their way forward to speak with someone. Someone, anyone. No-one was behind the desk. A man shouted, "Who's in room 1525?" and three people raised their hands. "1411?" Six hands. "801?" Four hands shot up. And that was that: the biggest spectacle of their lives was happening in an hour or less and they'd been had. They'd all been had.

Harrison let the elevator door close. He wanted his wife. He rarely wanted her—he had spent most of his life trying to get people, even her, to leave him alone—but faced with these two strangers, he wanted her more than anything.

"My mother is dying," Jean-Philippe said, kicking the heel of his moccasin against the elevator wall. "She is blind, and she is dying."

"Two of us could watch it from the balcony, and one from the window," said Claude. She looked at Harrison for support, but he had nothing for her, and stared blankly into her worried face.

Jean-Philippe shook his head. He hugged himself and clenched his teeth. "Could you two try the hotel next door?"

"No." Harrison's voice came out louder than he had intended. "No-one 's happy, but this is it. It's what we've got."

They both looked at Harrison. Occasionally he felt a pang of annoyance when he realized he was the smartest person in the room, and he felt that pang. Already, he had assumed the role of leader, troubleshooter, team captain, dad.

"All right," he said. The elevator doors opened and they stepped into the dim hallway of the seventh floor. "Let's each have a turn saying what we *intended* to get out of this experience. Then we can come up with some kind of compromise, some kind of plan."

But Jean-Philippe was already ten feet in front of them, his arms shooting out from his sides as he walked. Harrison looked at Claude. She was busy texting someone on her cell phone and clearly hadn't heard a word he'd said.

The room was as small as when they'd left it. Claude shut herself in the bathroom and Jean-Philippe sat on the formidable bed. He took the phone from the bronze statue's hand and di-alled his mother. For a moment, Harrison thought everything might be okay—two self-absorbed people wouldn't bother him very much, and he could enjoy the view from the balcony, while they watched from inside. He stepped onto the balcony and gripped the railing. The Estelle Hotel looked out over the ocean; the only thing separating it from the surf was a narrow pebbled beach. A few deadheads bobbed at the water's edge. People were setting up folding chairs and a cameraman was fiddling with his tripod, trying to get a solid stance on the rocks. Harrison could hear the dull hum of the gathering crowd but the wind was strong at the top of the hotel and mostly he could just hear the sea, the sound of a few screaming seagulls, and the muffled voices of other people on the balconies below. He had never seen the ocean devoid of ships. No barges, sailboats, fishermen, or speedboats, just the wide expanse of ocean, rolled out in front of him like an endless sheet of tinfoil. And then the kayakers arrived, and a few people in canoes, and soon the first 50 feet or so of ocean was filled with small pleasure crafts, their occupants passing flasks back and forth or sculling their paddles to keep the boats perpendicular to the horizon. It was getting dark.

Harrison had slept with his wife's cousin six months ago and had been trying not to think about it, but the weight of the act fell upon him and he was unable to rid it from his mind. He did not know if his wife knew, but he sensed that she did—not because her cousin would have told her (they rarely spoke, and lived a thousand miles apart), but because he'd always suspected that his wife could tell what he was thinking. He knew she sensed his attraction to Nadia, her cousin; he knew because she had drunk more than usual and avoided him for most of the night, preferring the company of a group of her brother's friends. They were gathered for her brother's thirtieth birthday, a big dinner party thrown by Harrison's wife and her mother in the regal and heavily treed backyard of her mother's home. Nadia was a surprise guest; she was visiting a university in the area, scoping out places to do a Ph.D. The attraction was immediate and overwhelming. Harrison hadn't felt that excited to talk to someone in years. He told her, at one point, that he wished he could talk to her forever. They fell away from the party and walked through the neighbourhood and up a steep hill that led to a little park with a view of the sea. It was almost dark, the horizon still partly lit by the setting sun. Their attraction was mostly made up of coincidences—they were born in the same seaside town, in the same month. They loved cribbage and okra and Brian Eno. She, too, loved to sail. Harrison told her he would take her out the following afternoon before she flew home. They walked back to the party, eager to say goodnight, to go to sleep, eager for it to be the next morning.

The next day Harrison left work at lunch, picked Nadia up at her hotel, and took her to the marina. It was a frigid afternoon at Fisherman's Wharf and almost no-one was around. Nadia wore a long coat with fur trim and white tennis shoes. They watched a man carry bags of groceries to his houseboat. The wind rustled the tarps slung over the sailboats, and the hollow sound of clinking masts carried from one end of the dock, where the fishing boats sat in port, to the other. Mick, one of the fishermen, had his foot propped on the side of his long-liner and was talking to his son Gord, who was slicing an octopus. Nadia and Harrison watched the boy dice the long, rubbery legs into small, purplish-white chunks. The air was bitingly crisp; a radio blasted Bon Jovi. Two dogs circled and paced, pawing eagerly at the entrance of the Fish Store, hoping for scraps from the young woman who worked inside, but she ignored them. One of the dogs wove between Harrison's legs and sat on his feet.

Mick motioned to Nadia. "Wanna see somethin'? C'mere."

Harrison shimmied his feet from under the dog and they followed Mick into the backroom of the Fish Store, where two white fish the size of area rugs lay sprawled on a steel countertop.

"Halibut," Mick said. "We caught 'em this morning. 'Bout 50 pounds a piece."

"They look like manta rays," said Nadia. "Or a couple of steamrolled beluga whales." They laughed and stared at the flatfish for a minute, their silvery, kite-shaped bodies face down on the steel.

"Love animals, do ya'?" Mick ushered them out of the room and joined his son on the fish boat. The octopus guts had been hosed off the floor of the long-liner and the rest sat sealed in plastic tubs. The wind gusted again and rattled the masts. Mick and Harrison had an understanding. He had brought women to the docks before.

"Why are you here?" Claude came out onto the balcony in a red windbreaker. She lit a cigarette, then offered one to Harrison. He took it.

"I wanted to see this alone." It was true. That was the only reason. A hotel room seemed like such a perfect escape. He had always wanted to do that—rent a hotel room for no reason—but never had.

"I didn't," said Claude. Her face betrayed years of drug abuse. Harrison hadn't seen a face like that in years—still beautiful, but so weathered. "I didn't want to see this alone. But who could I get to watch it with me? I got divorced two years ago, no children, my friends are all with their husbands, you know."

"Hm." Harrison hoped she wouldn't talk much longer. Already he felt tired.

"Where's your wife?" She tapped the metal band of his wedding ring.

The gesture made Harrison recoil, and he stumbled back into the hotel room, hit his ankle on the edge of the bed frame, and sat angrily at the end of the bed.

"I'm sorry," Claude said. "I'm really sorry. That was rude."

"Please do not *smoke* in here," Jean-Philippe hissed, and Harrison remembered his lit cigarette. He took a long puff and blew the smoke out the sliding door.

"My wife went to Yeoman," Harrison said. "With her mother and brother." He checked his phone to see if she'd called, or sent some kind of update—*stuck in traffic u were right*—but there was nothing.

Jean-Philippe pointed at the cell phone. "I'll pay you if I can use that—they say the phone lines will go out before the cell phone towers. I want to talk to my mother for as long as I can."

"Don't you have a cell phone?" Claude took Harrison's cigarette butt from him and threw it over the balcony.

"I lost it," Jean-Philippe said. He was a strange little man, Harrison thought. An angry little man. A hostile little man.

"You're welcome to mine." Harrison threw it at his chest and Jean-Philippe fumbled for it and it fell between his legs.

"I'm Claude." She thrust her hand at Harrison, and he shook it.

"Harrison."

Jean-Philippe flipped open the phone and studied it. "She's going to die any day. I was supposed to fly out this morning to see her, but they grounded the planes. No flights until tomorrow. She could die tonight, for Christ's sake." He paused and licked his lips. "The bill is going to be awful. She's in Quebec City—I'll get your address and send you a check, okay?"

"Okay," Harrison said. He went out onto the balcony. There wasn't a cloud in the sky. Some of the kayakers had tied their boats together and were eating sandwiches. The crowd on the beach had doubled and there were multiple film crews now, even a few in speedboats. A group of guys in an inflatable dinghy were singing Journey's "Don't Stop Believing" and drinking bottles of beer. He waited. He stood for what felt like hours. He listened to the tinny radios and the shrieks of children and a conversation on the balcony below about who would win gold at the Olympics, and he was alone. The wind off the water was cold, but it felt good to be cold, and it felt good to be outside. He forgot almost entirely about Claude and Jean-Philippe. He stretched out his hamstrings; he reached toward the sky. He cracked his neck.

And then Claude was at his back. "May I join you?"

He wanted, so badly, to say no. "Of course."

She shut the sliding door, and Harrison glanced through the glass at Jean-Philippe, who was walking toward them, gesturing animatedly, the phone awkwardly balanced in the crook of his neck.

"What do you do?" Claude offered him another cigarette and zipped up her windbreaker. She wore a tight-fitting black cap on her head and had put on fresh lipstick, a pale peach colour that stuck to the end of her cigarette each time she took a puff.

"I build yachts," Harrison said. "You?"

"I teach at the university." She nodded her head toward the room behind them. "What do you think his story is?"

"Seems like a rich kid," Harrison said. They turned and watched Jean-Philippe. The sky was dark enough now that they could see him, but he couldn't see them.

Claude cleared her throat. "I don't believe this business about his mother."

Harrison looked at her and smiled. That was it—that was why he hadn't felt anything for Jean-Philippe: he was lying. "I feel the same way."

"What's he up to then?"

"I don't know. Maybe I shouldn't have given him my phone."

"That business about writing you a check—"

"Crap, I know." He took a puff of his cigarette and looked at Claude's hands. They were small but strong looking, her short fingernails painted with rose-colored polish. She still had a white line on the finger where her wedding ring had been. She caught him looking at her, and they stared at each other for a minute.

"Two years goes by like two minutes," she said, tracing the white line around her finger. "I wear my ring when I teach. It's easier, somehow."

Harrison didn't know how it happened but Claude started telling him about her life—an abusive and philandering father;

51

a night in jail when she was seventeen; an ex-boyfriend who threw a knife at her head when she tried to leave him. He tried to figure out what he had done or said that made her think she could unload all of this information on him; he had always tried to figure out what it was about him that made people talk so much.

"—at this point I was used to someone leading a double life, and me having to bust them—" She was telling him what a good detective she could have been, how she could have been a private eye. She had spied on her father from an early age and uncovered a number of his affairs, proving it to her mother with motel receipts and phone charges. "I guess you just fake it until you're not faking it anymore. Right?"

But Harrison had lost track of the conversation and didn't know what she was telling him anymore. He turned back to the ocean, the great black expanse of it, and wished he were in one of the rowboats.

Claude lit another cigarette and pointed to a group of women on the beach, who were dressed in white, each wearing a wooden cross around her neck. "It took me many years to realize that some nights I just had to get through. Then more years still to realize that most people were already aware of this, wiling their nights away, watching movies, getting drunk, taking Valium or Ativan to make it through the long journey of the evening, do you know what I mean?"

He'd had girlfriends like Claude—talkers—and thought again of his wife and the wonderful daily silence they shared. She barely said a word. He suddenly found himself wondering why. Did something about him stifle her? She seemed able to bend in any direction to accommodate anyone—to match pitch with any situation—and Harrison wondered how far she'd had to bend to accommodate him.

"And now I find myself crying sometimes two, three times a day." Claude took a small glass pipe from her pocket, and packed the bowl with marijuana. "Smoke?"

"No, thanks."

She slid open the glass door and waved the pipe at Jean-Philippe. "Yeah?" she mouthed to him. She turned back to Harrison. "He's going to join us."

Harrison saw that her eyes were wet with tears. He stopped himself from putting his hand on her shoulder, and instead looked at the sky. A few stars were visible above the haze of the city. There was no moon. He couldn't see the boaters or the crowd anymore but he heard the waves lap against the hulls and the distorted music from competing radios. The couple on the balcony below was laughing. He heard the pop of a champagne cork.

"It could be hours still." Jean-Philippe slid onto the balcony through an impossibly narrow gap in the sliding door, and stood on the other side of Claude. He was right. The lights could appear at any time. It was part of the reason Harrison had decided on a hotel room. He didn't want to wait in the cold for hours. In retrospect, he wished he had invited his wife to join him. He wanted, desperately, for her to be with him now.

He had done his research. The auroras were caused by solar wind from the sun.

They would at first be barely visible. The display could last anywhere from a few minutes to hours and hours. He would see either a greenish yellow light or a red light (both caused by oxygen), or a blue light (caused by nitrogen), or, most likely, a combination of gases would produce purple, pink, and white lights. The more specific explanations—*why* and *how* this was happening—were difficult for him to comprehend. The Earth was surrounded by magnetic fields. So was the sun. A gigantic solar flare had occurred, brightening the sky at dawn that morning. Thousands of charged particles, called plasma, were shooting toward Earth at a terrific speed (most solar storms took between two and four days to cross the 93 million miles between Earth and the sun, but this one was travelling faster, even faster than the seven hours it took in 1859). The storm would reach Earth in twelve to fifteen hours, likely right after sundown. The key element in all of this—why it would be so spectacular— was that the magnetic fields of the plasma (called a coronal mass ejection, Harrison read) were in the opposite direction of Earth's. He tried to picture it as one rubber band hurtling toward another perpendicular rubber band, colliding and stretching, each affecting the other in some profound and electrical way.

It must have seemed like magic in 1859. Harrison read some-where that the sky was so bright over the Rocky Mountains that gold miners awoke and began making breakfast, thinking it was morning. In 1989, a solar storm knocked out the power in Canada for nine hours, but, beyond that, there was little anec-dotal evidence about what anyone could expect. In 1859, tele-graph lines had either burst into flames or electrocuted their operators. The most remarkable event, to Harrison, however, was this: some of the telegraph operators took the batteries out of their machines and were able to keep working using the elec-tricity coursing through the air. Harrison glanced at Jean-Philippe. Maybe he could talk to his mother—or whomever he was talking to—even if the lines were down. Maybe Harrison could call his wife just by thinking about her.

"Hit?" Jean-Philippe held out the glass pipe to Harrison, a lighter in his other hand. His eyes had glazed over. Claude rocked gently on her heels.

"No."

And then it started. It was as if someone had woven a thin green ribbon throughout the black sky. The little green snake traversed the horizon, paused and disappeared, its pale green tail intersected by seven white rays that shot upward from the hori-zon and spread out like a fan. The sky shone white. The crowd materialized beneath Harrison's feet—the kayakers, the children on makeshift rafts. It was so bright that Harrison could see to the bottom of the ocean, the sand beneath the waves, the rocks, bull kelp, and starfish all suddenly visible under a translucent sea. He searched his pockets for his safety glasses, his face hot. He looked at Claude and even she seemed paper thin, as if he could see right through to her bones. He fumbled past her and took his phone out of Jean-Philippe's hand. He could see through the plastic, into its intricate wires and microchip, its amazing metal skeleton. He dialled his wife's number and put the phone to his ear.

"Wake up," he whispered. "Wake up. Pick up." The phone was hot and Harrison had to hold it away from his face. He couldn't hear it ringing. It was as if the white sky had stuffed itself into his ears and expanded like a ball of cotton. He prayed his wife was safe. He prayed for it to be over. Claude finally grabbed the phone and tossed it over the balcony, where it began to smoke as it made its descent and collapsed in a pile of black ash on the ground. She reached into her pocket and squeezed a little bottle of hotel lotion over Harrison's burnt hand. Her cheeks were bright red and even with the safety glasses on she was having trouble seeing—she squinted, shielded her eyes, and finally pushed past Harrison and Jean-Philippe into the hotel room, where she sat with her head in her hands at the edge of the bed.

The people on the beach were grabbing their things and fleeing. A great surge of them pushed against the crowd, and Harrison hated that he could see it so clearly—the crush of bone through skin, a father holding his son above his head and not moving, letting the blows of the crowd fall on him, one after the other, while he stood his ground, holding his boy out of harm's way. And just as quickly as the white light came on, it receded. The crowd stopped. The air cooled. The black sky stretched out before them, lit with stars. One at a time, four points in the sky began to glow, uniting to form a crown of multi-coloured light. Bright pink, purple, green, and yellow light spun in front of them, leaving huge trails of gold ribbons moving like liquid silk across the sky. Harrison's ears popped and he could hear the auroras as they moved; they sounded like rushing water, like ice cubes shifting in a glass. The gold ribbons began to shimmer, and then it was as if the sun's light was being filtered through a giant prism, casting rays of magenta, deep purple, and sparkling white across the sky. Those who were not injured approached the water's edge again, and little by little, the crowd reformed beneath Harrison. The sky glowed green and all was still for a moment, and then, as if the wind had come up, the green liquid again began to dance. There were police officers now, and ambulances, and a man with a bullhorn was urging everyone to evacuate the beach and move inside. But no-one was moving. The sky was too beautiful.

"I—I—" Jean-Philippe's eyes were full of tears. Harrison looked past him and into the hotel room. The power was out and the room was black. He could see a faint outline of the bronze statue of the faceless man and the glowing ember of what must have been Claude's cigarette, but nothing else. He stared at his reflection in the glass for a full minute, then turned back to Jean-Philippe.

"I couldn't describe this if I tried," Jean-Philippe said. His gigantic Adam's apple bobbed as he spoke. "But I wish I could describe it to her."

"What is your mother dying of?"

"Emphysema."

"I'm sorry." And he was. Harrison could tell, now, that Jean-Philippe hadn't been lying. He looked back at Claude, but she was still obscured in the darkness.

"Let's take a drive." Jean-Philippe hurried into the hotel room, grabbed his Laplander hat and pulled it down onto his head. "Come on. Let's get out of here."

Jean-Philippe drove an old black Mercedes-Benz with a camel-coloured leather interior and tinted windows. Claude sat in the front and Harrison stretched out in the backseat. He was sweaty and panting from groping his way down seven floors of stairs in the dark. His knees were weak and his sides ached. The sky had turned a deep red and the air was still warm; had the sky not exploded in white light fifteen minutes before, the whole thing would have now seemed like nothing more than a spectacular summer sunset.

Everyone was still on the beach, and the city was empty. Jean-Philippe sped through downtown with remarkable deftness—Harrison felt as if he were in a car commercial, snaking through an empty cityscape in a sleek, black car. Within minutes they were on the freeway, headed toward Mount Yeoman, where Harrison told Jean-Philippe he could drop him off. Something was happening between Jean-Philippe and Claude—whether it was just that they were both stoned, Harrison would never know— and he was eager to leave them. Jean-Philippe ran his fingers up and down her forearm as he drove; his other hand rested lightly on the top of the wheel. The stereo played beautiful music. Harrison asked him what it was, but he didn't answer.

"It was a time in my life that has always been somewhat perplexing for me to recall," Claude was saying. "Jeremy, of course, but also with Alex. There are turning points, you know." She leaned toward Jean-Philippe and put her head on his shoulder and then Harrison could only make out bits of what she was saying. "...ultimately, though, having bad things happen to me has not made me a nicer person."

From then on, they were silent. Jean-Philippe nudged Claude off him, and she rested her head on the passenger window, presumably to sleep. He took off the Laplander hat and ran his hand through his hair, obsessively pushing strands behind his ears—his hair was just short enough that it fell to his chin the minute he took his hand away.

Harrison stopped watching him and looked out the window. The light show had, for the most part, ended, but an eerie green hue clung to the middle of the sky. They were ten minutes from Mount Yeoman. Harrison wondered if his wife would be gone by the time he arrived. He wondered if she was okay. He had been playing a strange game with himself since his early twenties—doing things to rid himself of guilt. He worked hard at his yacht business, harder than anybody, and each hour that he worked he imagined erased a sin from his past. He worked until his hands bled, then drove home and washed out all the yogurt containers, folded the newspapers neatly into the recycle bin, took the labels off soup cans, scrubbed the mould around the kitchen sink, vacuumed the car, hosed the floor of the garage, mowed the lawn, repainted the front steps, power washed the driveway. He went to the gym every day at six in the morning; he drank no more than two beers at any time. He ate very little meat, slept seven hours every night. He took vitamins. He flossed his teeth. No bill went unpaid. These actions absolved him. He did everything right; he did everything he was supposed to. And yet he had spent his whole life doing one thing, and then immediately wishing he'd done another. He did not want to help other people; he wanted only to be a good man himself, a man free of guilt and free of regret. It was a simple wish. He wanted, for once, to make the right choice. Instead he had done another bad thing, both to his wife and to himself, and nothing could erase it. He felt the whole weight of it, the weight of being a bad person. He sat in the leather-upholstered interior of Jean-Philippe's black car and let it sink into his bones.

Jean-Philippe stopped at a gas station just outside of town and tried to use the payphone, but the lines were dead. The power was still out, and they could see only what was illuminated by the car's headlights. Jean-Philippe's eyes welled again with tears and Claude held him against the payphone while he sobbed. Harrison paced the parking-lot and wished he had a cigarette. It occurred to him that no-one was around. He took a rock and smashed the glass door of the gas station's convenience store, reached in and turned the lock, and groped around in the dark until he found the till and the cigarettes behind it. He took five packs and fumbled his way out of the store again. Jean-Philippe and Claude stared at him in the bright of the headlights, horrified. He threw a pack at Claude and she caught it awkwardly with both hands. Her face was groggy from sleep and her hair had fallen out of its bun and lay in a pile on her shoulders. Her windbreaker was tucked under her arm. She had on heeled sandals and stood almost as tall as Jean-Philippe. He, too, looked tired. Big tears gathered in his eyes and fell down his face as he stood there, looking at Harrison and the packs of cigarettes in his hands.

"I think she died. I can feel it." He let go of Claude and stood pigeon-toed, then wrapped his arms around his body. "I feel different."

Harrison's arm throbbed and he saw that he had cut it on the glass door. It was a superficial wound, but already it had soaked the cuff of his denim shirt and was bleeding still.

Claude pointed at the sky. Three ribbons of light were weaving their way across the sky, like white curtains blown by the wind. "Come on," she said. "Let's watch the rest of it."

Harrison eased off his shirt and wrapped it around his arm, then took Jean-Philippe by the shoulders and led him toward the car. He felt thin and frail in Harrison's hands. Harrison put him in the backseat, gently, as if he were a child, and reached around his body to fasten his seatbelt. He started the car and drove back onto the freeway. The beautiful music began again and Claude took off her seatbelt, climbed into the back, and took Jean-Philippe's hand. Harrison rolled down the window and felt the warm air on his bare chest. When they reached the top of Mount Yeoman, he parked the car beside his wife's station wagon and left Jean-Philippe and Claude to watch the sky. They sat on the hood of the Mercedes, arms around each other. Jean-

Philippe's Laplander hat rested on his knee. Claude tucked his hair behind his ears and held him as he wept. She called out to Harrison as he walked away but he pretended not to hear.

He found his way to the small path that led to the lookout. The lights overhead were as bright and clear as a thousand moons. He was not walking toward atonement; he knew he had failed his wife and always would. She sat with her mother and brother on either side of her, on the bright blue bedspread they used in the guestroom. They were drinking bottles of beer. Harrison's wife had on one of his old sailing caps and her brother's jacket. Her legs were tucked under her, and she'd taken off her shoes. There were grackles in the trees and they called out to one another, diving from tree to tree in a great swarm. Harrison's wife loved birds. She was pointing at them and trying to mimic their calls when she saw him, and he must have looked like a mad man, bare-chested, a bloody shirt wrapped around his arm, a pack of cigarettes in each of the pockets of his jeans, and a lit cigarette in his hand. She looked at Harrison, and he saw that she was happy to see him—her face brightened into the most beautiful, childlike smile.

"Hi," she said. She stood and took the cigarette from his hand, and inhaled deeply. She was half drunk. She peeled the bloody shirt off his wrist and stared at the wound.

Their first night together, they moored at Friday Harbour and after dinner sat in the cockpit of Harrison's sailboat—a wooden Thunderbird then—and he showed her that by disturbing the surface of the sea with their hands, they could make visible the phytoplankton, the small electric bodies glowing like stars. "It's called bioluminescence," Harrison said, taking her hand and trailing her fingers through the water. Her hand was stiff in his and she pulled it out of the water quickly and wiped it on her jeans. She was cold and so they moved into the boat's cabin and Harrison made up the v-berth so they could go to bed. It rained that night and the boat leaked and they woke at dawn, soaking wet.

Harrison and his wife stood under the black sky, flickering green, then white, then gold. They watched the final moments of the lights together, and he picked up her hand and traced the path of the last ribbon of light with her fingertips, their hands

moving from one side of the sky to the other, until the light receded, then finally disappeared forever.

Into the Blues
Kathryn Mulvihill

It was the summer of 88 and me and Tom had big plans. We'd just started working at his old man's drywall operation, hauling four by twelve sheetrock boards and learning how to tape and mud and sand. We mostly worked local jobs in the big fancy houses going up all over here in the hills. Still do today.

One sweltering afternoon we were sitting out back of our latest job site, at a picnic table, in the shade, eating lunch. The sky was clear blue and the river was glassy without a lick of breeze coming off of it. I pulled one of the brochures on sail fishing charters I'd picked up at a travel agent in town out of the back pocket of my jeans and slid it across the table. "Check it out, Tommy."

Tom glanced at the brochure, then looked down and kept eating his sugar pie.

"Hello, earth to Tom."

He wouldn't look up.

"Tom."

He gathered up the wrappers from his pie and chips and sandwich, shoved them back into his lunch bag, crumpled it all up in a ball and pitched it down toward the shore.

Then he pulled out his smokes and zippo, lit up, took a big drag and gave me a look.

"I don't think I can go on the trip, Bob."

I slapped the table. "Good one. Like you got something you'd rather do than get drunk and catch marlin?"

He didn't say anything. Just gave me that look.

Shit.

"I'm saving up for a down payment on a house," he said quietly, looking down over the water.

I half choked on my bologna sandwich. "What? Are you for real, man?"

"For me and Bridget." He was shading his eyes now, looking south toward the dam.

Man, was it hot! "Christ Tom, don't you think it's a bit early for that kinda talk?"

"I love her, Bob."

This was unbelievable. For the first time in our lives me and my best friend of sixteen frigging years were actually making serious cash and he wants to go off and get married. Shit. "Don't you wanna live a bit before you settle down, Tom?"

He looked at me and his eyes were tired. "Look, I know you're still getting over what happened with Manon, but this is different."

I felt winded. Why did he have to bring that up? I grabbed the stupid brochure and started fanning myself with it. "She could have at least dumped me before she started screwing that university jackass."

"I'm gonna ask her to marry me, Bob."

Shit. I pulled a beer out of the cooler, held it against the back of my neck for a few seconds, popped it, downed half in one gulp. "So you're telling me you're cancelling our trip? Is that what you're telling me?"

"Look, I'll talk to her, see what I can do."

What a fucking joke. "Talk to her? Don't you mean "Tell her," Tom? We've been planning this trip since Grade 8."

"Bob."

I felt like someone punched me in the gut. "I'm serious, Tom. You gotta make a stand right away. Look what happened with me. I did backflips for that girl."

"Bob. She's not telling me what to do."

"Then you're saying it was your idea not to go to Mexico?"

He looked hurt. "Look. I'll talk to her."

"Oh, for fuck's sake! I'm going to go jump in the river. This heat's killing me."

Fifteen minutes later Tom's old man was standing on the big second floor deck yelling down. "Break's over boys. Get a move on it. We need that new section sanded and all those sheets in

62

the back of the truck hauled up here before you go."

I couldn't stop thinking about it all afternoon, but I didn't bring it up again. We were covered in sweat and drywall dust by three, our usual quitting time, so we jumped in Tom's rusty old F150 and headed straight to the Petro Can to pick up beer, gas, ice, worms, chips and wine coolers for the girls.

Old Rose Brown, the ancient cashier, with wild long grey hair and coke bottle glasses, all crippled up with arthritis and wheezy from asthma, who'd been working there since all of us could remember, said the same thing every day. "Where's the party, boys? When am I gettin' my invitation?"

Tom had a soft spot for old Rose because she helped him win Bridget's heart. One warm afternoon in early April, a baby robin fell from its nest wedged over the light fixtures and lay sprawled on the concrete in front of the store. Rose scooped it up and took it inside and nestled it on a towel in a cardboard box. Tom and me blew into the store just when Bridget and her kid sister Abbie were at the cash oohing and aahing over it.

Rose watched Tom watching Bridget. When the girls left, she smiled and nodded to Tom and held out the baby in its box. "Take it and look after it, Tommy. Trust me."

That evening, Bridget and Abbie showed up at Tom's house with a styrofoam container full of nightcrawlers.

"We've come to feed the baby," Bridget explained.

Tom nearly had a fit. He'd been pining over her since Grade 6.

The girls named the baby Lucky and spent that whole evening feeding it worms. Tom didn't know what hit him.

He said Bridget just kept smiling at him and said "I didn't know you were an animal lover, Tommy."

When Tom took his Swiss Army Knife and cut all the worms in half for the girls so they didn't have to rip them, Bridget leaned in and gave him a big kiss on the cheek. The rest, as they say, is history. Ever since then Tom and Bridget were joined at the hip and he had a huge shit eating grin plastered on his face. Talk about annoying.

After stocking up on supplies we headed over to Townline Road to pick up the girls and Tom's younger brother, Jimmy, at Dynamo Ranch. They all had jobs mucking out stalls. Boy, did they stink!

Both the girls were crazy about horses. Especially Abbie. Took that job even though she was so tiny it took her twice as long as any of the other kids to muck out a stall. Abbie always was a little different. Spent half of Grade 9 in the loony bin. But she sure was pretty. Jimmy couldn't take his eyes off her.

Bridget squeezed in practically on top of Tom, then Abbie squeezed in next to her and me and Jimmy sprawled in the back seat and sparked up a joint.

"Who wants a toke?" Jimmy held the joint over the seat.

"No thanks. Pot makes you stupid," Bridget said looking at Tom.

Me and Jim made faces and rolled our eyes at each other in the backseat.

In about ten minutes we pulled up at the girls' place. Abbie and Bridget's mom had this super rich boyfriend who docked his kick-ass bass boat up there that spring then whisked their mom off to spend a drunken summer in Europe.

When Bridget first showed us the boat, Tom looked real serious and said "it'd be a shame to waste a beauty like that."

We had a routine. As soon as the girls made the sandwiches and we'd gassed up and stowed the cooler, fishing rods, tackle boxes and boom box we'd squeeze into the boat and head up near Banana Island to go for a swim and wash off the day's grunge. We'd wade around on the sandbar, basking in the blazing late afternoon heat, blasting tunes, splashing each other and swimming. Bridget rode around piggy back on Tom the whole time. Then we'd cruise around, up and down our stretch of lazy river, from one dam to the other, fishing, drinking beer, smoking pot.

That particular night, when the sun turned orangey over the hills, the heat started to break, and the fish started to bite, we were jigging for walleye in one of our secret spots where a weedbed grows up right in the main channel. All five lines were in, jigs floating about a foot shy of the bottom. The girls actually liked fishing as long as it was catch and release.

Jimmy was sitting dangling his legs over the bow, sneaking glances at Abbie who was swivelling around leaning back on the post seat with her eyes closed singing "She got a smile that it seems to me, remind me of childhood memories...."

Tom was sitting in the stern on the other post seat, tying on Bridget's jig head. "Maybe we'll get our first house on a little lake, eh Bridge? Nice little fishing spot?"

Bridget was standing behind Tom with her arms around his neck. She didn't say anything, just put her chin down so it was resting on his head.

I was chilling in one of the comfy middle seats, sipping my beer, flicking caps at a squawking seagull that was flying around divebombing whenever I tossed a chip in the water. I was trying not to think about Mexico.

Bridget turned and gave me a dirty look. "Stop it! That's cruel, Bob."

"What? Who cares about shit hawks? They're not even real birds."

"Yeah, we used to shoot shithawks with our bb-gun, right Tom?" Jimmy piped up.

Tom turns around, gives me and Jim the eyes.

I tossed a few more chips.

"Stop it. Tom, tell him to stop." Bridget had her scrawny arms folded across her chest now, facing us, ready for a fight.

I was just getting ready to throw some more chips when next thing you know, "Fish on! Fish on! FISH ON!" Jimmy's rod was bent double. Big action.

Jimmy got busy reeling and I passed over the net. He scooped up a decent sized fish. "Oh yeah, it's a blue, boys. We're into the blues." He's so excited he almost falls off the bow. This was the first school of blues we'd hit all summer.

For two girls who'd grown up on the river, Bridget and Ab sure didn't know much about fish.

"What are blues? Is that the fish making that squeaking noise? Bridge can you hear the noise it's making?" Abbie was leaning in, peering over the landing net. Jimmy reached in with the pliers, pulled the fish out by the jighead lodged in its mouth then violently snapped his wrist and slammed it into the water.

Abbie leapt back. "Oh my god, Jimmy! What are you doing?"

"What? I'm taking the fish off the hook. How else am I 'sposed to get him off? "

"Well you could wiggle the jig out with your hands like you do with other fish, Jimmy. And you could be more gentle. You don't have to be so cruel." Bridget's whining is really getting on my nerves at this point.

"Yeah, how 'bout you try taking your fish off the hook with your own hands, Bridget?" I down my beer and grab another out of the cooler.

Tom was giving me a dirty look now. "Bridge, he can't. They have barbs. One on their back fin and one on either side fin."

"Yeah, the barbs sting like crazy!" Jimmy has already re-baited his hook and thrown his line out and now is lying along the bow, head and shoulders over the edge, scooping up water, wiping worm guts off his hands.

"Still there's no need to throw them in the water so hard." Bridget was glaring at me.

But her nagging was cut short. We'd drifted into a big school of blue cats. Couldn't keep them off the lines. It was practically a fulltime job just passing the landing net, the pliers and the worms back and forth.

We kept at it for a good hour until we finally got bored and the mosquitoes got really bad, then we called last fish.

Jimmy ended up with the last fish and it just so happened to be a huge channel cat. Thing must of been twenty pounds. Not long after he chucked it back in the river he said "Hey, why don't we noodle up here? Our channel cats get big too." He's got a beer in one hand and one of those electronic badminton racket things that fries bugs on contact in the other and he's waving it around wildly. Zap. Zap. Zap.

"Hell yeah. That's the best idea you've had all year, Jim." I held my beer out toward him as if to make a toast.

"What's noodling?" Bridget said with a certain tone.

"We could start a whole new trend boys." No way was I gonna let Tom's bossy little girlfriend of three fucking months shut down an opportunity like this.

"No-one does that up here, Jim." Tom's slamming his lure against the water, stripping the worm off of it.

"Yeah, what's noodling?" Abbie was swaying trancelike to the music and waving her towel around trying to keep the bugs away.

"It's just a way of hand fishing our dad told us about. Our Uncle Stirling used to do it when he worked down in Louisiana." Tom said warily.

"Yeah it's an old native trick," Jimmy said. Zap. "You gotta feel around with your hands and feet." Zap. Zap. "You come to a hole in the bank you stop and feel around. Zap. You come to a big log on the bottom, you stop and feel around." Zap. Zap.

"You mean you have to go in the water?" Abbie asked, eyes wide. "What if you get stuck down there?"

Jimmy couldn't contain himself. He stood up held out his arms and wiggled his fingers screaming "And your fingers are the bait. Right, Tom? Right?"

That got Bridget's attention. "Excuse me? What? "

"Um, Yeah, you find a nest and you wiggle your fingers around and get them to go for your hand. It's very, um, humane, uh, 'cause you don't even have to use a hook." Tom was shooting the old puppy dog eyes over at Bridget when he's saying this, but it clearly wasn't working.

"That's disgusting." Bridget rolled her eyes and turned away from Tom.

"And then what, Tommy?" I could tell Tom was into it.

"Well, hopefully they bite for your fingers." Tom said quietly. He was looking at Bridget's back.

"Then you grab him and pull him out with both hands and there ya go! Zap. Zap. Zap. You got him!" Jimmy yelled.

Bridget turned back toward Tom and said loudly "I don't want to noodle. You're all drunk and it sounds stupid and gross. Come on, Ab, let's go for a swim." She tossed off her baseball hat and started stripping down to her bikini.

But Jimmy's practically jumping out of his skin at this point. "Explain how they nest, Tom. Say how they nest." Zap. Zap. Zap. "Tom!"

It took Tom some time to tear his eyes away from Bridget and swivel back toward me and Jim.

"Umm, yeah, they're amazing. Yeah. Um. Yeah, the male hollows out a nest in a mud bank, under a log, in an old tire, whatever."

"Yeah, the male makes a nest. The male does all the work, right Tom?" Zap. Zap. Jimmy's jumped in beside me in the other middle seat. He starts pulling beer out of the case and lobs one to me and Tom then cracks one for himself. Zap. Zap. Zap. Zap.

"For Christ's sake Jim, would you put that fucking thing down!" All I can smell is charred mosquito and pot. I pass him the joint I just lit.

Jimmy laughs and takes the joint. "Tom, the nests."

Tom's smiling. "Yup. That's right. The male lures a female there to lay her eggs." He takes a big swig of beer, then looks around quickly, leans in and takes the joint from Jim.

The girls are swimming behind the boat now and Bridget is yelling things.... "I feel like skinnydipping. I think we should all go skinnydipping!"

Tom passes the joint back, swivels toward the girls.

"Once she lays her eggs, he boots her out then guards the nest. He'll go more than a week without eating till the eggs hatch. Right, Tom? Jimmy's kneeling on his seat, bouncing. "Right, Tom? Those suckers are starving!"

Tom swivels back, takes the joint again.

The conversation continued in this way until we came to the conclusion that July was the right time of year for spawning this far north and that the mouth to Green's Creek must be chock full of huge males guarding nests.

"C'mon Tom, we should give it a whirl." If we weren't going to Mexico, I sure as hell didn't want to pass up an opportunity like this.

Tom looked at me, then over at Bridget. I could tell he was into it, but he didn't say anything.

"We got a good hour and a half of light left," I said.

"I don't think Bridget's going to go for it, Bob."

"I think if you want to do it, that should be good enough, Tom. Me and Jim sure as hell do."

"Yeah, Tom, come on. Why do you have to do what Bridget says? When I get a girlfriend, I'm never going to let her tell me what to do. That's for sure."

"We'll see." Is all Tom said, looking doubtfully toward the girls swimming.

"I'll pay 50 bucks to whoever gets the first fish." I was shamelessly pulling out all the stops. Neither Tom nor Jim could resist any kind of bet, especially when it came to fishing.

But Bridget wasn't budging. The girls climbed back on the boat. Bridget was wrapped in a towel, pulling her hair into a pony tail. "Absolutely not. I don't want to noodle."

"Well, okay, sure, you don't have to Bridge. Us boys'll just do it," Tom said.

"No. You're all drunk."

Jimmy and me and Abbie all went up to the bow of the boat and turned the other way, pretending to look at the sun set. It was flaming orange over the hills and just starting to descend.

"What do you mean, no?" Tom had a slight edge in his voice now.

"It means no you are not going noodling. It's disgusting and dangerous and that's it."

I snuck a look at Tom then, and I smiled. I could tell he wasn't just going to lay down and do what he was told, especially with me and Jim there. Instead, he said quietly, "I say we take a vote."

I didn't waste time. "Yeah, let's take a vote. Everyone who wants to go noodling raise their hand."

Bridget sneered at me.

Naturally, all the boys raised their hands.

"It's our boat," Bridget said smugly, looking pointedly at Abbie.

Everyone looked at Abbie. She flushed red and kept looking from Bridget to Jimmy. Her T-shirt was clinging to her wet bathing suit and she couldn't have weighed more than 90 pounds.

Jimmy had a flash of brilliance. "Abbie, if you vote yes, I'll muck out half your stalls every day for the whole summer."

Bridget looked stunned. She sulked the whole way down to the creek. By the time we made it into the wide muddy bay she was giving all of us the cold shoulder. Even Abbie.

Us boys played rock, paper, scissors to see who got to go first. Jimmy won. We decided the best place to start was the eastern edge where there was a nice clay bank about a hundred metres long or so. We anchored the boat and Jimmy stripped down to his shorts.

Bridget made one last attempt. "You'd really take advantage

of a poor creature nesting? You'd really do that?" She was looking at no-one in particular. She looked like she was going to cry.

Tom looked at Bridget pleadingly and all he said was "Ah
c'mon Bridge." Then he turned to Jim who was just climbing
into the water. "Jim, remember to use your feet too. But try not
to stir up the bottom too much."

Bridget clenched her jaw and didn't say anything.

Now it was my turn to be smug. "Yeah, c'mon Bridget, Tom
and Jimmy have been fishing since they were two years old.
Fishing's in their blood."

Bridget looked confused. "Huh?"

"Alls I'm sayin is, you knew Tom was a fisherman when you
decided to go out with him."

She narrowed her eyes and said icily "Based on what happened
with you and Manon, Bob, you should be the last person giving
out relationship advice."

That felt like a knife to my gut.

Then Tom turned and gave me a quick pleading look as if to
say, okay, that's enough Bob, please don't make things worse.

So all I said was, "I'll make it an even hundred for the first
fish."

Jimmy started screaming, "Oh yeah, a hundred bucks man.
A hundred bucks on first fish!"

Things went wrong right off the bat. The bottom must of
had a foot of sediment on it which made walking difficult and
visibility impossible. It was deeper than we thought right off
the bank and was easily two feet over any of our heads which
meant Jimmy had to stay submerged when feeling around for
nests. So Tom decided he would go in with Jimmy to give him
a hand.

After about twenty minutes of feeling around blindly, they
came upon the perfect location, a huge log lying on the bottom
nestled horizontally along the bank.

Jimmy was so excited he could barely contain himself. "Oh
yeah, this is it for sure! Get your camera ready, Abbie. Here
comes a hundred bucks boys. Get yer hundred bucks ready
Bob!"

They decided that Jimmy would go down alone and Tom
would float on the surface overhead just in case Jimmy needed

any help landing the fish.

Jimmy came up and took some breathes and rested for a minute then said, "Wish me luck boys," and down he went.

Then he came up and yelled, "I found a nest! There's a big hole right under the middle of the log!" and down he went again.

We waited for what seemed like forever but he didn't come up. We could see bubbles and lots of movement in the water but the water was so cloudy we couldn't see him. So Tom went down.

Then Tom came up, took a big breath, yelled "We need your help, Bob!" then went back down. Again we could see lots of movement, but they didn't surface.

The girls were freaking out. "They're drowning! Help them, Bob! Bob help them!"

I have to admit, even though I was pretty drunk, I was panicky too. I dove in, clothes and all and swam to where they went down. I found them right away. I grabbed the waistband of the first pair of shorts I found and hauled them up to the surface. It was Tom.

"Get Jimmy! His hand is stuck and it's biting him."

I went back down, found Jimmy right away and hauled him up. He didn't appear to be stuck on anything any more.

Now they were both up, and oh my frigging god, what a bloody mess. Both of their hands were cut up all to hell and bleeding all over the place. I had to haul them both onto the boat.

They both started wandering about the boat in shock, bleeding, babbling.

"What happened? What happened?" everyone kept yelling.

"It must of been a snapper," is all Tom kept saying. "A huge fucking snapper."

"Tom, sit down!" Bridget points to the bow seat and start ripping up a towel, wrapping his hands, tears streaming down her face. "Someone help Jimmy! Abbie, go help Jimmy!"

"I got my arm stuck in the hole and it kept biting me." Jimmy is flailing his arms and blood is flying everywhere.

"I can't. I think I'm going to be sick." Abbie is looking at Jimmy in horror. She looks like she's going to pass out.

71

"Jimmy sit down! Bob, go help Jim." Bridget picks up another towel and throws it toward me.

Tom is too wound up to hear anything. "Then I stuck my arms in to pull Jimmy loose and it started biting me. It was cornered. That must of been one huge motherfucking snapper."

The poor girls. There was a lot of blood. I mean a lot. There was blood everywhere, on the seats, the deck, all over the cooler, our clothes. The boat looked like a war zone.

We finally got them all wrapped then we got outta there fast and drove up to the hospital in almost total silence.

We ended up waiting thirteen hours in Emerg up in Wakefield. Tom and Jim were bloody messes, Abbie had to be sedated she was so hysterical and Bridget sat like a statue and barely said one word the entire time.

It must of been a full moon because even though it was a week night the ER was packed with cottagers and locals. A bunch of kids drove off the road on the bad curve on the 366 in La Pêche and came in by ambulance. That set us back by hours.

Poor old Rose Brown was brought in by her brother Adam. She was pale as a ghost and her asthma was so bad she could hardly breathe.

"It's the heat." Her brother said. "The heat is the worst." He sat with his arm protectively around her.

One of the Charbonneau boys from over on Connell Road was there for what he thought was a broken foot from dropping a rock on it. "You guys are gonna get those rabies shots *esti*. Those snappers get the rabies from eating the muskrats. They fulla the rabies. Yur gonna hafta get those crazy huge needles in your stomachs like every day for like a month *tabarnac*. My uncle Rémi he ad to get that. Hurt like hell like."

Bridget got up and went for a walk at this point.

It took a couple of hours just to get into triage. Neither Tom nor Jim could use their hands, so I went with them to fill out the forms.

Bridget sat with Abbie who hadn't stopped crying and rocking in her chair the whole time. All she kept saying was "I thought they were going to die. I thought they were drowning."

The triage room was kitty-corner to and within earshot of the waiting-room. The door was left open when we went in and I could see Bridget in the waiting-room from where I sat. "*Two* of you got bitten by a snapping turtle?" the nurse said, very loudly, looking over her glasses as she handed me a clipboard with the forms. "And how exactly did that happen?" Bridget was staring at me as if so say, yeah, how the fuck did that happen, Bob? Jesus. I looked back to the nurse.

She at least got the boys bandaged up pretty good so they weren't seeping so much blood anymore. But she seemed like she was enjoying it. The interrogation part. "So you were feeling around for catfish under a log, is that right? You were submerged under the water, is that right? I guess you didn't have access to a fishing rod?"

The whole waiting-room was cracking up when we got back. Well everyone except for Abbie and Bridget that is. Abbie was still sniffling and Bridget was sitting, ramrod straight, pretending to read a Reader's Digest.

Rose was smiling though. "Sounds like quite a party, boys," she wheezed. "Youse boys is regular river rats you are. Regular river rats." She exploded into a huge coughing fit then, but her eyes still had a glint in them.

The doc stitched up their hands and said they were lucky they didn't lose any fingers. By the time we dropped off the girls it was getting light out. Bridget still wasn't talking.

After that, things weren't the same with Bridget and Tom. They stayed going out for a few weeks more, but they were just going through the motions. Then in August she announced out of the blue that she'd been accepted to UBC and would be leaving in two weeks to start a degree in biology. Tom didn't even know she'd been applying to universities. It sure took everyone by surprise. Even Abbie.

The worst was that Tom didn't even hold it against me. The whole noodling thing—me convincing him to do it I mean. He's not like that. All he kept saying was I really loved her, Bob. I really, really did. At that age I never believed you could know you loved someone so fast like that, but now, I know different. When I met my Ange, I knew I loved her the minute I laid eyes on her. Like a zap of lightening straight to my heart. Life's funny that way. From one minute to the next you never know what's going to come along and knock you flat on your ass. Like when Bridget left. Or like a couple of months later, when the accident happened.

Tom still counts his lucky stars that Jimmy pulled through. The doctors called him "miracle boy." The cops said their parents were killed instantly on impact, said they never felt a thing. The paper called it one of those "freak accidents." They were out muskie fishing on Thirty-One-Mile Lake. Tom didn't go. He stayed home to mope about Bridget. It happened when they were cruising in for the night. Jimmy was sitting in the bow, like usual. Thank god their mom always made them wear life jackets. Their dad was sitting in the stern steering the 9.9. Their mom was in the middle. Their dad never did get around to fixing the nav lights.

When Jimmy finally woke up and came home from the hospital, he struggled through all that rehab, and then he tried and tried to get his Grade 12 but he just couldn't do it. So he came to work for me and Tom. We'd taken over the drywall business from Tom's old man. He does all right. It's been well over ten years now and his speech is pretty well back to normal and his balance is much better. He'll never run the show, that's for sure, but he's fine as long as he doesn't have to deal with clients and he sticks to his routines. The best thing is, he gets to spend most of his time with his two best friends in the whole world and he'll never, ever, have to worry about work. Not around here. Those big, fancy houses just keep going up. It's never going to slow down. There's enough business in these hills to keep us boys busy hanging drywall for a lifetime.

The Land Below
Alice Petersen

The last two parties of the day saw no adult albatrosses at all, so it was up to Rae to make sure that the visitors did not go away disappointed. She tried to create the missing birds, making huge gestures with her arms in front of the audiovisual display, dramatising facts about the dangers posed by drift net fishing, and the sly thieving nature of stoats, but nothing compared with a glimpse of a white wing sweeping around the headland where the Otago harbour meets the South Pacific. You couldn't conjure it: it was, or it was not. Well, at least the tourists got plenty of pictures of the two fat chicks on the windy hillside, wisps of down fluttering at the back of their necks.

Just after five o'clock she hung up her vest and took her handbag out of her locker.

"Well that's it then. I'll see you on Monday, Sheila."

Sheila looked up from the statistics on her screen.

"You okay, Rae?"

"Yes, thanks, just a bit tired I suppose."

Rae brushed the back of her hand across her eyes. She was glad that Sheila had come to work at the albatross colony. A constant kind of friendship had grown up between them, based on having been at school together. To know someone at thirteen is really to know them. She remembered the greeting they had shared on Sheila's first day, as if it had not been 30 years, but just a long summer holiday since they had seen each other. Rae walked over the car park and down to the railing at the cliff's edge. A gull in red stockings ran before her, skirting the puddles full of pink sky. Below her the cliff fell away in a cascade of fleshy ice plant starred with orange flowers. When she looked back she saw Sheila waving as if she had something to tell her. Rae walked back up to the building.

"Rae, I was wondering if you'd like to go to Sandfly Bay tomorrow afternoon, to watch the penguins come in?"

"I thought you usually worked on Saturdays?" Rae searched her pockets for her car keys.

"Not this Saturday. Interested?"

"What time?"

"About three?"

"Sounds good."

The two women hugged. Rae could not remember how they had fallen into this hugging. It had started as a New Year thing, but each time they held on a fraction longer. It was only a matter of time before they would look each other in the eye afterwards and one push away a loose strand of hair from the other's face.

As Rae swung in and out of the bays along the harbour road back to Dunedin, the sun crept up the hills behind the city. The street lights had come on by the time she turned into the driveway of the villa on the crown of the hill. She locked the car. The air was sharp on the lungs and hazy with smoke from the wood fires down in the valley.

On the floor inside the front door lay a familiar packet addressed to her mother, postmarked from France. Rae picked it up and threw it onto the kitchen table without looking at it. She knew what it contained: Gauloises, the annual reminder of the year that her mother had spent at the Sorbonne before marriage claimed her.

Rae took down her mother's apron from the hook beside the stove, found matches and relit the pilot light. In the days when everyone was switching to electric ovens, her mother had insisted that gas gave better heat. I'll make Dad some scones, she thought, thinking of her mother's floured hands turning and tossing the dough as if she were slapping laundry on a rock, then throwing the trays into the oven through a crack in the door as if a volcano might billow out into the room. There was nothing her father liked better than scones and raspberry jam. Making jam had been one of the last things her mother had done before they left to spend New Year's Day with the Leamings. Just after a quick stop for tea at Catcher's Hotel, while the Leamings waited to greet them with leftover Christmas pudding and honey-glazed ham, Rae's father lost feeling in his left side and slumped forward over the wheel. The car veered across the road into a power pole.

It was always surprising how few pots of jam came out of a batch. All that washing and picking through, taking out the mouldy and the squashed, and they boil away to nothing. Rae found a jar at the back of the cupboard and tapped on it. The cellophane seal was concave and tight as a skin.

While the scones cooked she turned over the package on the table, looking at the French stamps. Rae knew so little about her mother's life before her marriage, especially the mythical year when she studied at the Sorbonne, boiling eggs in a kettle and sleeping in a hat, scarf and black mittens. Each year the French flatmate, who must now be heading for 70, sent a packet of Gauloises to New Zealand. The cigarettes would arrive squashed, battered and stale, yet without fail Rae's mother would retreat to the bottom of the garden where she would smoke one or two each afternoon for a week. Rae and her father raked the leaves into piles around the unseeing woman wreathed in smoke.

Rae went about the house picking up bits and pieces that might help her father to pass another moment in the nursing home where the floor polisher hummed night and day in the corridor. She found a newspaper cutting about the retiring dean of the medical school, and an article about a giant squid found floating on the surface of the sea.

The physiotherapist was in the room when Rae arrived, putting away the mirror that she had been using to encourage Rae's father's left side to move. While Rae watched, her father succeeded in twitching his thumb a fraction.

Rae's father was a retired medical man. He enjoyed his golf, and he enjoyed sitting in front of the television diagnosing the weather lady's goitre problem. There were no mysteries for Rae's father. The body was a machine, a bundle of processes, and like a car, it could be fixed. Rae's mother, on the other hand, had been a machine that could not be fixed. *I'm sorry Ms. Small, there is nothing we can do.* Nothing we can do. There's always something you can do. There were always scones to make, shirts to iron.

Dr. Small chewed laboriously at a scone, pronouncing it delicious. There were crumbs and a coffee stain on his jumper. They talked about the coming election, about snow in the forecast.

"If only I could get out of this darned chair," he said. "You will look after the house after I'm gone, won't you? Don't let them change anything."

"Oh Dad, you mustn't talk like that."

"Well I'm not going to last forever, but your mother wouldn't like it if they changed things around." Rae thought of the mottled red carpet and the gas heater with the plastic logs and the revolving bulb that flickered inside them. There was everything to change. It was a young couple's renovating dream.

"Don't worry," she said.

"Forget what I said about staying in the house, Rae. Sell it. You have your own life to live."

An old hot vein of frustration opened up in Rae. She took a deep breath.

"It's all right, Dad. Don't worry," she said.

On Saturday afternoon Rae and Sheila met in a farmer's field high up above the Pacific. A sharp wind blew the macrocarpa trees further into their ancient stunted shapes. Signs pointed visitors over the paddock toward the giant sand hill at the entrance to the beach, warning them not to bother the lambs. Rae took off her boots and rolled up her jeans. The two women picked their way down the sand hill, eyes narrowed against the wind, both remembering their thirteen-year-old selves on a school outing, launching themselves off the top of the hill with whoops and bounds. The sand hill seemed smaller now, trodden down. At the bottom the wind-blown sand stung their ankles and hissed in the tussock. The beach was empty, except for a sandy piece of driftwood that developed flippers and a pointed nose, and lumbered off into the dunes. Sand had banked up against the sea side of the bird hide and they both had to work to get the door open.

"My feet are so cold, I think I'm going to die!" Rae pulled her socks out of her pocket and used them to rub at her heels. "I don't know why I took my boots off in the first place," she said.

"Old reflex, I suppose," said Sheila. She opened the shutters, letting in a thin sliver of shoreline and the winter sky. "I haven't been here for years."

"Me neither," said Rae.

Rae sat on a bench in front of the window, and Sheila turned and lifted each of Rae's feet in turn. She brushed the sand off matter-of-factly as if it were not Rae's foot at all, but a piece of drift wood that she had picked up to take home.

"Better?" asked Sheila.

"Yes, thanks," said Rae.

A penguin paddled in the waves just offshore, craning its neck to see whether the coast was clear. Soon another joined it, and soon there were three. When they felt safe they reared up off their chests like little toys and waddled toward the shelter of the flax bushes, inching their way up the hillside on their private tracks. The women sat side by side on the narrow bench, no longer touching, not Rae, not Sheila at all, just two women who had driven out to watch the penguins come in.

I wonder how long I can carry on not being me? Rae thought. *This isn't me. Or perhaps it is me, but not a me that I know yet. I must see if Dad's nails need clipping.* She tucked the thought away, the same way her mother used to come in from the garden tucking stray wisps of hair behind her ears.

Rae could feel Sheila's palm warm against her ear, silencing the sea, leaving only the sound of her blood.

"You should look after yourself, you're looking a bit thin," said Sheila. Rae was silent. "You okay Rae?"

"I don't know about this," said Rae.

"What's there to know?" asked Sheila.

What was there to know? Only the agapanthus and the empty clothesline.

"Rae, come and stay with me for a while. Let me look after you for a bit. No, that's not what I mean. Come and live with me Rae, we'd be good together."

It was as easy as that. *We'd be good together.*

"Thanks, Sheila." Rae looked at Sheila's small, perfect earlobe, unable to look her in the eye. "I'll think about it, I really will."

"Do," said Sheila, placing a hand on each of Rae's shoulders. "Promise me you will." She kissed her on the cheek.

They left the bird hide and walked back toward the car. They passed only one family coming the other way, two adults and a child who ran in and out of the sea, oblivious to the cold waves.

"You don't have to go home, Rae. Come to my place."

"Thanks, I know I don't, but I always go up to see Dad about this time."

"I'll see you on Monday then?"

"Yes, I'm in from 11 until 4."

The numbers defined the space between them. Of course Rae would see Sheila. There was work to do. If a life together were to be arranged, it would be thought out with the practicality of grown women, of egg sandwiches and a thermos of hot water, of teabags in a separate container. It could wait until Monday. They got into their cars. It was a relief not to be buffeted by the wind any more. Rae drove home past the spiked silhouette of a cabbage tree against golden sky, and a lone sheep, watching.

Rae went up the path to her parents' house, past the hydrangeas with their wet mottled leaves. *I don't know how to proceed at all from here*, she thought, *and I should. I am a middle-aged woman.*

It was getting late. She picked up the package from the kitchen table. The postmark said Toulouse. She found scissors and carefully slit the brown paper apart. Inside was a packet of cigarettes, unsealed and then resealed. She pulled the cigarettes out. There was no note, but on each cigarette a single French word was printed: plain, domestic words that ordered and re-ordered, told a different tale each time. *Monday, coffee, bed, chair, cheese, blanket, Wednesday, bread, Burgundy, Thursday, grass, cemetery.* One cigarette had initials on it, her mother's maiden name, K.M. Rae thought of her mother smoking random dreams at the bottom of the garden. Over time the famous year in France had fragmented into single words, brittle as shreds of old tobacco. She looked at a cigarette that said L.F. de R. for a long time before she put it in her pocket.

It was getting late. Rae ran a bath and got into it before the enamel had finished warming up. She lay there until the water was nearly cold, occasionally flapping her hands over the surface of the water. She thought of Sheila in her waxed jacket doing battle against the wind, the wind lifting her curling hair away from her forehead, her profile dark and intent.

Women do it all the time, pack up, leave, move in with their pastoral care officers, their nutritionists, physiotherapists, local health food coop owners; women who touch their skins and minister to their bodies and minds. Daily, thousands of women arrive with squashy bags full of sweatshirts at the front door of a place that isn't yet home. There was nothing to it. But how could she do that, if she did not really know what she felt? Why was it so hard to feel anything at all?

She dried herself and dressed and went out to find a few things in the garden to take up to her father. Rae's mother had loved flowers, but not in an ordered way. The garden was filled with masses of nodding aguilegia seeded in clumps. The dried sticks of the flower heads stood above the scarred and dying leaves. Rae clipped some late heartsease and looked at their inquiring faces, wondering what her mother would have said about her father being in a home, and what she would have said about Sheila.

Rae's father had been at medical school with Sheila's father, so it was assumed that the two girls would get along. At school Sheila had been an aggressive hockey player, often getting called out for having her stick raised too high. She was at her best at school camps, making bivouacs and jumping into cold rivers with her clothes on. In class she fought with her teachers, struggled against their facts and their requirements, and their sheer stupidity. Her burning anger with the world gave her a kind of power. Many of the girls felt it and avoided her.

Not long after Sheila started school, Rae's parents invited Sheila and her father to lunch. Sheila had been patently bored. When the adult talk turned from fire alarms to stomach cancer, the girls asked to be excused. They went outside, following the path into the orchard. The quince leaves hung motionless in the warm autumn air, and walnuts in their twisted black cloaks lay ready to be picked up off the ground before the rats that lived in the hedge could get at them.

One of Rae's chores was to gather up the cooking apples and put them in a basket in the corner of the kitchen. On Friday nights, Rae's mother would sit behind the scales, slicing the apples with a firm hand. Rae had not collected apples for days and a strong wind had scattered them on the ground. Sheila picked up an apple and threw it against the garage wall. The apple hit the bricks with a satisfying thunk, split in two and dropped off, leaving behind a few fragments. She picked up another and another, smashing the apples against the brick wall with fierce joy. *Sheila is happy*, thought Rae. *Sheila is having a good time at my house.* She felt proud to be pleasing Sheila when no-one else could, so she stood and watched while Sheila went about gathering all the apples from the orchard and even pulling some off the trees and throwing them against the wall.

On Sunday afternoon Rae's mother was raking leaves for a bonfire. The smoke lay curled about the trees.

"Will you look at what those boys have done to my apples? It's a crying shame. All my apples." She pointed at the bruised and smashed fruit lying under the garage wall, the brown fragments clinging to the bricks.

"That's terrible," said Rae. She went inside to learn her French verbs. For a while after the apple incident, Rae avoided Sheila in the school corridor.

Rae sat in the chair on the porch and looked out at the grey lines of the sea. On Monday she would make her lame excuses to Sheila, and their friendship and everything else would be broken. All she could think of was the sadness in her mother's voice as she looked at the smashed apples. And in the same voice she could hear her mother asking, *where is love in all this?* Except that her mother had never said anything of the sort.

That afternoon she found her father in a sombre mood.

"It was my fault, Rae. I killed her," he said.

"Dad, you had a stroke. There was nothing you could do."

Rae's mother had died shortly after her arrival at the hospital. It was a blessing, everyone had said so.

"Dad, I'm thinking of going away for a break. Just a fortnight. Will you be all right without me? My friend Sheila says she will look in on you. You remember Sheila's father Rex Haworth from medical school?"

"Fine physician."

Rae had no idea whether Sheila would agree to it.

"So where are you going off to, Rae?"

"Mum's cigarettes arrived the other day, and I thought I might go to France." She tried to make it sound as casual as going to the beach.

"That's a long way from here. What do you want in France, dear?"

"I want to tell that French woman about mother."

"Who?"

"You know, the cigarette friend, the flatmate from the Sorbonne."

"Well you're not going to find her, dear," he said.

"Why not?"

"Because it wasn't a woman."

"It wasn't a woman?"

"No. I think you'll find it was a chap." With difficulty Rae's father turned his head and looked out the window.

"Oh," said Rae.

She turned and looked with him out at the wet rhododendrons. Raindrops were making their way down the pane, separating and colliding and separating again. So change was possible, even after death. Deep inside Rae a great bird lifted off and the land below fell away. She was high above the white caps and there was no sound but the wind.

"Will you be all right, Dad?"

"Yes. No. I don't know. You go on. I'll still be here."

"Dad, are you sure?"

"I suppose so. Does this Sheila friend of yours make scones?"

"I'll ask Dad, I'll ask."

Hour of the Crab
Patricia Robertson

Kate, walking along the beach, found the body. She was kicking pebbles into the little frothy waves and pretending. Each stone bore away a burden. *Unswept snow grit on our front steps. Stupid argument with Vikram before I left. Missing the wedding, and my mother saying*—. The last pebble thunked against something sodden. There in the shallows, a few strides ahead, some tangle of something—washed in by the tide, probably. Sunlight glittered, darkening her vision. A larger wave flung the tangle closer, wrapped round a dead fish.

Not a fish.

A human foot, bloated, grey-white. Jeans plastered to thin legs. Now an arm, swollen, wound in seaweed.

She stopped on a caught breath, watching without hope for the betrayal of tiny movement. Only the waves moved, rocking, rocking. Hand over her mouth she bent forward. The body was slack, without tension, T-shirt holed and rotting. Narrow shoulders, flat chest—not a child but not quite an adult, either. She slid her hands under the ankles and staggered backward, grunting. It was heavier than she'd expected. The frilled edges of a cut on the left calf gaped.

Along the avenida the first of the cafés were clattering their metal fronts open. Shakily she looked up and down the beach. No-one except, far off, near the rocks, holding a scoop net, an elderly fisherman who would not know English. The head lolled toward her—a face that was not a face, lips eaten away, teeth and nose coated with foam. She knelt, eyes half-shut, peeled the pockets apart. No ID, no cellphone, nothing. The zip of the jeans, salt-crusted, gave suddenly on a fat bleached penis. A man, then—boy, really. She hadn't been sure.

Where had he come from? He must have been in the water for days. On the more intact foot was a tattoo of some sort, a stick figure—was that it?—with a triangle on either side. She puzzled over it. Smuggling? Drugs? Or nothing, just some design he'd liked. But if she went to the police, here in the Mediterranean south.... A sand crab scuttered from the right ear.

She'd go back to the pension instead, wake Gavin, go for coffee and keep her mouth shut. Let someone else find him. It wouldn't take long. Gavin especially—he'd finished his medical residency the year before, he often worked nights in Emergency—Gavin deserved a break. She couldn't do a thing for the drowned boy, but she could protect her husband. Hadn't that been the reason for coming here—to leave the weight of duty and a just-ended Canadian winter behind?

When she reached the shop where she and Gavin had bought ice creams the evening before, something stopped and turned her. He was someone's son, after all. Someone's brother, or lover. Somewhere people were worrying about him. The row of cars parked in front of the Comisaría, bearing their sword and axe symbol, made her hesitate. She crossed to the other side, as if they were watching.

—Yes, yes, we find on beach all the time. At the Comisaría, when she finally managed to get herself inside, the officer interrupted her flailing Spanish. —We pick up and make report. Shrugging, all stubble and rumpled shirt, his hands splayed out. —The body, it goes to *el depósito de cadáveres*.

All the time? They found bodies on the beach all the time?

—He is migrant. Illegal migrant. He was exasperated, half-contemptuous. —They come in boats, too full boats, from over there—the hand flung out again—from África, Marruecos, Tunicia, and engine breaks, they have no food, no water. Then maybe a storm comes. He pushed angrily at a stack of papers.

Not drugs, then, but desperation or determination or reckless desire. *We pick up and make report*—a statement that was not callous but exact. It wasn't the officer's fault he'd come, or anyone's. In an hour or two there'd be no evidence the body had ever been there. Other people would lay down their own living bodies on the sparkling sand.

—You went for a walk? This early? Gavin was already in the bar next door to their pension, coffee and some thin biscuit on the table in front of him. Male heads swung in Kate's direction, then away as she sat down.

—I thought a walk would wake me up. She felt the prick of tears. There'd been her father's cancer, just last year, all over in seven weeks, then Gavin's brother, suicidal when they'd axed his support job at the group home. Force it down. —It's beautiful out there. No tourists at all. The barman lifted his eyebrows at her, mimed the raising of a cup.

—What do you think *we* are? Teasing, eyes softening in his sleep-creased face, hair on one side still flattened.

—Not like those—oh, *you* know. The Marthas and Henrys. Their own term for the fat ones impaled with gadgetry, the overloud voices. A pretence, really; a private snobbery.

—You look—I don't know. Subdued. Washed out.

That was the trouble with marriage; once you peeled apart from each other, you were seen through. But then she'd been told all her life she had an honest face.

—What about a swim? Near that thatched bar?

He meant where they'd been the day before, soon after they arrived. Not a hundred metres from where she'd found the boy.

—You go if you want. She shut her eyes and drank the last of her espresso quickly. —I'll finish unpacking. Get my things hung up.

—Come on, Kate. Out with it. Did *I* do something? He slumped back in his chair, deflated. —I thanked you, didn't I? For getting us here?

On the beach the boy sat up suddenly and smiled at her, his white teeth alarming. —I am sorry, I fall asleep. It was long, to swim here. He looked out across the water toward the opposite shore.

—You *swam*?

—After boat sinks. His small dry laugh sounded as if he were choking. —I have to, no? He stood, his body narrow and bony under the wet shirt, the ratty jeans. —I am Hamid. From village in Rif Mountains. People come, buy *a*—he closed his eyes, searching, made the feminine shape of a pitcher in the air. — You are from America?

—Canada. She glanced away, breaking eye contact, reassuring herself with the glint of glass from the avenida. —Can I—I don't know, take you somewhere?

He turned, following her gaze, seeing—what?—in the glass and traffic. —Ahhh, Canada! He said it as if it was some mythic place and laughed softly. He didn't need help, then. He seemed fine. —*I* come to find life.

—You mean a living? she said, puzzled. —Make a living?

—No. A life. Over there—he jerked his head toward Africa—is nothing. Walking to meet you.

She could never have done what Gavin did, watching people die. As a child her sister had buried mice and sparrows in the back yard; Kate, repulsed, stayed in the house, cutting little suits out of upholstery fabric for her dolls. Now she designed furniture made from recycled materials for an energetic local business called BioHome. Her mission in life was to invent the perfect chair. Make people feel cradled, held, utterly safe. She saw her chairs stationed in every boardroom on the planet, bringing peace, happiness, good will.

She'd done a past-life regression once; Gavin liked teasing her about it. Apparently she'd been an eighteenth-century Spanish nun, a member of the Discalced Carmelite order, no less, founded by St. Teresa of Ávila.

—A nun! Let's see, your father was Jewish, your mother's lapsed Greek Orthodox—

—In the eighteenth century, Gavin. It doesn't matter what I am now.

—Why is no-one ever reincarnated as a cleaning woman? Or a—I don't know, a coal miner. Or a mugger.

Both of them had had progressive childhoods. Gavin's grandfather had been a union organizer in Winnipeg, a member of the Communist Party, and in the forties had learned Russian as preparation for moving the family to Moscow. The Stalin show trials had eventually dissuaded him, though Gavin, as a small boy, had called him Tovarich—Comrade—Gramps. Kate bore the marks of a different set of convictions. She'd been named Katharina after her Orthodox grandmother, Anna after her Jewish one—all those A's!—and became Kate-Anna, then simply Kate. Her mother's mother, the Katharina, had made a pilgrimage in her seventies to the monastery whose saint's name she shared. It lay at the foot of an Egyptian mountain where, so it was said, Moses had received the Ten Commandments. Kate's grandmother had seen with her own eyes, in a hollow in the granite, the imprint of a sandalled foot.

In the afternoon she pored over the local English-language newspaper, *The Andalusian*. Properties for sale (beach-front flats, expat businesses), the arrest of a fish-and-chip shop owner for speeding, water restrictions because of the drought. Nothing about drowned migrants—oh yes. One small paragraph, near the back. A boatload of refugees, the third this month. The engine had broken down in rough seas, they'd drifted for days. Thirty-nine out of 83 had been rescued. The dead included seven children under four, their bodies thrown overboard by their parents. —Where are my babies? one mother kept asking the Red Cross workers.

Had *he* been on that boat? Somewhere in the continent beyond people waited for news. Waited to hear if he'd arrived safely, if he'd met up with others, if he'd found work. When she looked up the boy was sitting there, leaning forward on his elbows, watching her as if she were deciding his fate. *Stop it,* she wanted to tell him. *Stop following me. It's your own fault. You chose to come.*

—D'you suppose they were Senegalese?

They were sitting outside the bar near the pension, Gavin staring at the ocean dazzle, still in his sand-caked swim trunks, she still holding the newspaper she'd read aloud from when he came back from the beach.

—They could have been from anywhere in Africa, couldn't they? Running from civil war or something.

—Sub-Saharan migrants, it says here. That man in the market back home, what's his name, Abdourahim. He says he couldn't find a wife in his village. The rich men take three or four.

She was tearing the story out, the paper soggy from her sweat-damp hands. —He offered me a necklace. Asked would I marry him. I *think* he's Senegalese.

—I've no idea, I've never talked to him. His tone was of someone speaking, with infinite patience, to a child. —Look, Kate, don't you think you're being rather morbid? It's horrible, but there's nothing we can do, is there?

Morbid. Morbidity. One of Gavin's medical terms. Death expressed as the frequency of disease in a population, as a set of statistics. Except that, set against individual lives, the statistics broke down. You couldn't measure human life that way. The boy himself would have been outraged, or perhaps merely resigned.

—I wasn't going to tell you. But I found this—dead person. On the beach.

He came again that afternoon. She was walking along the street. This time his ragged T-shirt, peculiarly, bore the Toronto Blue Jays logo. *Je m'appelle Joseph*, he told her. He was from Chad, from the capital, N'Djamena, where he'd had his own small tailor shop until what he called les difficultés broke out. The second time rebel groups destroyed his shop he'd decided to flee. A cousin in Marseilles had sent him the money. He was 22 years old. He'd left behind a wife, Maryam, and two small children. —*Il fallait que je vienne*, he said, spreading his hands wide—it was necessary that I come. He did not smile.

—They didn't say anything else? The police?

—They find them all the time. They weren't interested.

Gavin, fiddling with the rope bracelet round his wrist, looked up at her, squinting in the blond light. —I'm sorry, Katie. Really. Sorry you had to go through all this.

But what had she gone through, really, compared to the boy? Gavin had summoned the hot coal in her throat, the one she couldn't swallow.

—They must take them *somewhere*. The ones who survive, I mean. Maybe someone else on the boat knew him.

—But even if. His fingers paused for a moment. —I mean, what's the point?

89

None, except that she was being followed, hounded even, in a way she didn't understand and couldn't have explained to Gavin. —I bet they'll know at the pension. It's a small town. There must be a camp or something.

—And then what? The line of his cheek was concave with disapproval. —Spend your holiday holding hands at some detention centre? Anyway, it'll be heavily guarded. They won't let you in.

Where was the Gavin she knew from home? *He always listens, your husband. Really listens, not like the other doctors.* She stood up, a sleepy leg tingling into life.

—You don't have to come with me if you don't want.

—It's a vacation, Kate. You kept telling me that, over and over. Remember?

The camp, it turned out, was miles away—the woman at the pension gestured vaguely up the coast—and out of bounds, just as Gavin had said. But there was a place, the Centro de Refugiados, that helped them, though what sort of assistance they gave the woman couldn't say. She regarded Kate with disapproval, as if Kate herself had brought the migrants. The woman who ran the Centro was Catalan, from Barcelona, did she know? Did she know about the Catalans and their separatist sympathies? No, of course not. Only in Spain did such nonsense occur. Only in Spain were they allowed—but the telephone rang and she swung away, glaring.

The Centro was a 30-minute walk through untouristy back streets. By the time Kate rang the bell on Calle de la Gloria, the damp flannel of late-morning heat clung to her back and armpits. After a long wait, footsteps, then the grille in the door sliding open. Kate attempted an explanation.

—A moment, please, said a female voice, in overly enunciated English, and a deadbolt grated. —*Pase, pase.* I am Victoria. The top of her vigorous curls came not quite to Kate's chin; the hand with its tapered vermilion nails was as small as a child's. —We are firebombed a few months ago. That is why the lock. She laughed as if it was all a joke. —I used to be journalist in Barcelona. Catalan and a *migrante* sympathizer—that is two for one, no?

In the heat Kate had become slow and baffled. —You find body, yes, I understand, Victoria said firmly, and took Kate's arm. —The police go to beach every morning to search for. This one came after they left.

In the tiny office upstairs she pushed Kate into a chair, gently, as if dealing with an invalid. —I am sorry. Very—what is word?—disturbing. I know.

—There's a camp, isn't there, Kate said, and held the glass of cold water Victoria brought her to her forehead. —Where they process people. The woman at the pension told me.

—And why do you care? Victoria said without rancour, sitting on the edge of her desk. —It is not for sightseeing. For taking photos.

—I don't—I mean, shouldn't I? Shouldn't everyone? She took a deep, shuddering breath; there wasn't an answer. —I had to. That's all.

Victoria grunted deep in her throat, like an animal. —They escape, if they can. It is like a jail only worse. Then there are others, they arrive, no-one sees them. She turned and pointed through the window at the hills above them. —Up there they are hiding. Many, many. Her English seemed to be slipping further in the emotion of the moment. —In the trees, in caves. It is shaming, *vergonzoso*. Not right.

Before coming they'd pored over the pictures of the Alhambra— the tilework, the filigree, the sunstruck fountains. The names that came from some jasmine-scented dream: the Court of the Lions, the Hall of the Two Sisters, the Gate of Pomegranates. A belated honeymoon, Gavin had joked; they hadn't been able to afford one when they'd married four-and-a-half years ago. Though the truth was it had been built by Christian slaves.

—We'll catch the *AVE* train in the morning, it leaves at ten. Arrive just in time for lunch. He touched her arm lightly, which she understood as an apology. —We could have a picnic in the gardens.

—Why don't we go the day after tomorrow instead?

—Oh, for god's sake. The guidebook landed, with more force than necessary, on the bed between them. —It's that camp, isn't it.

—There's others, too, in hiding. I think if I went back—

—It isn't just about that boy. It can't be.

—It's about—. Would she know, if she went? If she met them all face to face? —You go, if you want. It's okay with me. Really. Maybe we can go again, later on.

—There's nothing—you don't even speak the language. He flung up his hands incredulously, like the police officer. —Oh, hell. The hell with it. I'll go on my own.

They took her in the Centro's dusty van. Victoria and someone called Javier—thin, stooped, a wedge of black hair above his glasses—who turned out to be a graduate student studying sociology and community development at the University of Málaga. —We are all part-time, here at the Centro, Victoria explained. —We get money, little bits, from the *parroquía*, parish I think you say, from other organizations, from people on the street even. That exploding laugh again. —The cathedral was a mosque, long ago, before fifteenth century. So it's appropriate, no, to give back to Muslims?

And what did she do when she wasn't here? —I am with the migrants. Actually I am married to one. She grinned at Kate's startled look. —Not these migrants. Earlier ones. People forget.

He was Czech, apparently; his family had escaped in '68, after the Soviets invaded. She inclined her head, ironic. —Victoria Beltrán Sokol, *a tu servicio*. Vojtech has his own law practice. Very useful. She pressed a thumb downward in the air, pinning some squirming prosecutor. Drove fast, one small foot flooring the accelerator, while Javier shouted history from the back seat.

—Five years ago almost, we find, me and my brother, we find bodies, like you. At another beach, more east. He jerked his head in the direction of the dust cloud swirling behind them. — Eleven. Yes, eleven, all at once. So we form, me and Luís and his girlfriend—

—Ex-girlfriend, Victoria corrected, swinging the wheel hard—a huddle of sheep billowed round the curve. She raised an eyebrow in the rearview. —Really, Javi. Such *ancient* history.

—We are support group, also pressure group, Javi said, unrepentant. —We bring food, clothes, find doctors. Try to change laws. The road, surly, was twisting itself higher into the hills; Javier caught hold of the back of Kate's seat as Victoria took another curve with abandon. —Now more come, all the time, some people say is our fault. I tell to them, okay, what you want? We take them back to beach and push in water?

—At first we try to find jobs and apartments. So they can become legal. Victoria threw up a voluble, despairing hand. —All are traumatized. And no-one wants them.

They were still climbing; Javier, turning, pointed to the glitter of sea far below them. —Many end up down there. That is biggest cemetery. And it has no *lápidas*—Victoria, how do you—?

—Tombstones, Victoria said.

They pulled into a sort of rough clearing, high up in the pines. As Kate got out the cold air shocked her into wakefulness. Children in various stages of undress were appearing between the trees, holding plastic bowls and bottles. A clump of them stared at her in silence; others chattered round Javier, tugging at his sleeves. Victoria bent down and picked up a small girl in a dirty pink dress.

—Khadija had a birthday last week, didn't you, Khadija? Victoria held up three waggling fingers. Khadija pulled her thumb from her mouth and held up three of her own, smiling uncertainly. Beyond the children dim adults moved, shadows in the deeper shadow. Plastic sheeting had been strung up here and there, bits of cardboard wedged underneath to make walls.

—Can you imagine, Victoria said. —Living in the hills like this, eating squirrels and sparrows. She shrugged, turning the gesture into a jaunty bouncing that made Khadija giggle. A kind of stupor hung over the place. Javier, children still hanging from his arms, dispensed bandaids and aspirin to a few adults, their faces guarded, expressionless. —You are here, they are more cautious, Victoria explained.

A tall greying man in too-short pants, his face an ashen black, stepped forward. —This is Nagmeldin, Victoria said as Kate held out a hand he didn't take—from fear? Embarrassment?

—He is from Sudan. God knows how he got here. He has told us different stories. Nagmeldin said something in Spanish;

Victoria snorted between her teeth. —He thinks you are some government official. I explain you are tourist.

A tourist. A Martha, even if she wasn't fat and loud. One of the lucky ones, the ones who'd won the lottery of birth and lived across the ocean and ruled the world. She put her hand behind her back, overcome with shame. Why had she come? And how could she describe, respectfully, that disfigured body lying at her feet on the sand? She looked about for a stick and knelt, drawing what she remembered of the tattoo in the loose earth. Nagmeldin squatted, hands on knees, staring, murmuring, while Victoria translated.

—There were many young men on his boat. From Sudan, most of them. He says this—Victoria pointed to the drawing— is not from Sudan.

Nagmeldin rose in one uncoiling movement and began speaking, hands animated—something to do with papers, documents. He was 39, too old to have come here. Back home soldiers had killed his wife, his four children, two of his brothers. Home, in fact, no longer existed. He shut his bloodshot eyes and opened them again. —He thinks you have come to offer jobs, Victoria said.

—Let's ask someone else. Javier retrieved his arm from a small boy, nostrils clogged with mucus. —Jamila, maybe—she knows everything.

An old woman in a head scarf, one arm shrivelled, squatted on the ground, stirring something over an open fire. —We bought them camping stoves but they don't use. Victoria, lips thinned in exasperation, pointed to blackened trees at the edge of the clearing. —Last month a shelter burns. Three of them go to hospital, then the police deport. We are lucky no-one dies.

Kate bent and drew the tattoo on the ground again. Jamila nodded vigorously, jabbing her finger as her husband, small and rheumy-eyed, explained in some mix of languages. —Berber, they say, Victoria said, straightening. —From Morocco, like them. But not on a boy. Only Berber women have tattoos.

—An illiterate boy from the mountains. The woman who spoke, in startlingly fluid English, stood apart from the others, a tall figure enfolded in a miraculously clean shawl. —The er-Rif Mountains, in the north. Perhaps you know of. Glancing at Kate with contempt, face thin and alert.

—He was on your boat? Kate said, suddenly riveted.

But the woman flung a fierce look at Victoria instead. —Why does she care? What is this boy to us? She pulled the shawl tighter, outlining her swollen belly. —The sea took my husband, does she know that? Does she know this child has no father? Her bangled arm swung recklessly round the encampment. —The dead, at least, are at peace. But the living.... Who cares about us?

Into the silence Javier stepped forward, offering oranges and milk to the crowd around them. Khadija, given the important task of carrying food to her family, staggered off, beaming. The tall woman folded the items in her shawl with offended dignity; Jamila, still stirring her pot, spat on the ground.

—Can you tell us more? Victoria said quietly. —About this boy?

The woman lifted her shoulders, evidently wearied. —My husband tell me to hold onto boat, I don't know how long, many hours. A fishing boat saves me. We had nothing, no food, nothing. Too many people. The boat tips over.

—And the boy? Victoria said again, so softly Kate could barely hear her.

He had been among other people at the port, waiting to cross. The men teased him about his woman's tattoo. Along with many others he had boarded some patched-together thing riding low in the water. What had happened to them she had no idea. When Kate asked for his name she flapped her hand, as if brushing off flies. The tattoo had been his mother's idea, to protect him from *jnoun*—the evil spirits that entered the body from the ground in a strange country.

—*Azemmur*, Jamila said suddenly, insistently, pointing at the drawing again. —*Azemmur*. The husband said something to the woman with the shawl, who listened with a kind of angry indifference.

—They say it is olive tree, she said, staring at something beyond them all, above their heads. —Olive tree between two mountains, for strength. In Arabic only is true name. *Al-zeitun*. Didn't everyone know the olive had been brought from Syria in the eighth century by a young Arab prince? He had fled Damascus after the slaughter of his entire family and had founded Al-Andalus—Andalucía, the very land where they stood.

On the way back Javier drove; Victoria sat slumped in the back seat, hands filled with scrawled notes, photographs, even a résumé, written in what turned out to be badly spelled French. She and Javier talked desultorily in Spanish, of which Kate caught only the odd word: *una semana, claro que sí, nada más*. She turned toward the back seat when it seemed, for a moment, opportune. —Who is she, that woman? Why's she here?

Victoria opened her laptop and began tapping something into it. —She is from wealthy family in Fez. Educated, her father is professor. Victoria squinted at one of the strewn notes, then tapped some more. —Zainab, her name is. She is supposed to marry but she fall in love with cousin. Poor cousin. They run away. Now she want to go back, but she know her family will not accept.

There she stood, wrapped in her shawl, holding her milk and oranges above her belly, her face angry and astonished as if she hadn't expected the world to fail her so dramatically.

—Tomorrow, Javier said, we organize a big dinner. We take food and cook with them. You want to come?

She couldn't risk another argument with Gavin. Besides, they were going to a fiesta in a village further along the coast whose name she didn't remember where villagers in authentic costumes re-enacted the Christian conquest of the Moors.

—How many people survived from Zainab's boat?

—Who knows? A muscle in Javier's jaw flickered. —Maybe the police catch others.

Victoria, behind them, gave another of her animal grunts. —Police hold for 60 days, if they find, and then they deport. The grunt changed to a snorting laugh. —And then there is Zainab. She *want* to go back but she cannot. Ironic, no?

Two AM and she couldn't sleep, though Gavin was snoring lightly through his open mouth. This time his name was Drissa and he came from Mali. He was seventeen years old. He wore a faded green shirt that was far too big for him and rope-soled sandals. He'd spent twelve days in a boat trying to reach Spain;

he was hoping to get a job in the vast plastic greenhouses along the coast. His father was dead, his mother ill, he needed money to support five siblings. With his high cheekbones and insouciant smile, Europe, beckoning and golden, would open its arms and embrace him.

The replacement bus, when she boarded it that morning—the usual one was out of service—had sprung seats and a defeated air. Across the aisle an elderly woman in black pulled her head scarf over her face Arab-style as Kate sat down. She'd left Gavin a note telling him where she was going. Envied him his ability—honed at his job?—to leave it all behind, to sleep as if he deserved it. Well, he did, didn't he?

Despite two *cafés solos* she felt foggy and dislocated. A crucifix swung wildly from the rearview on each hairpin curve, providing apparent absolution, though she already knew she'd arrive safely. Azemmur, as he now was, was depending on her. From the Málaga bus station a taxi bore her through the gold varnish of late morning, needling in and out of heavy traffic. The red Moroccan flag with its five-pointed star hung from a nondescript building in a street filled with consulates—Serbia, Luxembourg, Yemen.

—We arrest those who profit from such trafficking, the consul told her, a tall and dignified man in his precise European suit. He seemed to believe she'd travelled all the way from Canada to correct this wrong, a misapprehension she couldn't alter. —Also we have campaigns on TV, warnings. His finely lashed eyes closed and opened again. —But they think we are lying. They believe those who came earlier, who maybe were given amnesty. He had decided she was there not to find a name but to lodge a complaint. Tourists, especially North American ones, needed to be appeased, to be comforted like children. She laid before him the tattoo she'd drawn on a piece of paper.

—Yes, yes, it could be an olive tree. It could be anything. He shrugged. —I grew up in Casablanca, I went to l'Institut d'Études Politiques in Paris. These—he pushed the paper back to her—are village beliefs, you understand. I have no knowledge of such things.

They occupied the same world, she and the consul. They lived in one world and the boy and Zainab and Nagmeldin in another, and there was no bridge between them. Gavin, sensible Gavin, must be driving, elbow resting on the open window, along the turquoise coast, past those miles of greenhouses under plastic, to that village where they pretended to murder each other with swords and scimitars. She was almost out the door when the consul called after her.

—Go to the port. There are Moroccans working there. Someone might be able to help.

A bulky man in a hardhat and safety vest came toward her, eyes performing a practised flick down and up her body. Two o'clock, oppressively hot, men and equipment unloading a container ship tall as a skyscraper, the *BF Leticia*. The smell of oil, rubber, hot tar.

—I'm looking for someone, she shouted over the clangs and rumbles. —Someone who might know a boy from the Rif Mountains.

The foreman, if that was who he was, grinned, white teeth impertinent. —You don't know village? In those mountains are many villages. He struck the drawing lightly with his fingers, contemptuous, suspecting something, something sexual; his nostrils flared, avid. —How you know this boy?

—I found his body. On the beach. He came in one of those boats.

The nostrils contracted; the man stared, taken aback. —I call Marouane. Okay? He is from er-Rif.

Marouane could not have been more than fifteen, wiry and underfed; an eyelid flickered nervously. Men went looking for work, he said, from all the mountain villages—from Azilane and Akchour and Abou Bnar. Brothers, cousins, uncles, now scattered through Germany, Spain, France. In some of the villages only women and children were left. He knew nothing about some Riffi man with a tattoo. If he had died, then Allah had willed it. He stared at her, astonished that an American could travel so far and know so little.

Gavin was in the bar next door, his head turned, like the other men's, to the TV and the soccer game. The fiesta had been won-

98

derful, he said without moving; she should have come. People dressed in jewelled turbans, silver armour incised with crescents, or wearing white tabards with red crosses, carrying dragon-emblazoned shields. The captain of the Moors rode a real camel through the streets. A commercial came on; Gavin, turning, was exuberant, still caught up in the game. —Stupid, that argument, he said. He was being contrite, generous—the Gavin she knew again. —We can go back if you want. The village. It's a pretty place.

He didn't ask about where she'd been. Perhaps he didn't want to know. The hot coal had cooled and slid downward, lodging in her stomach.

—Would you mind? she said. —Another day on your own? I have something else to do tomorrow.

He stared at her, eyes narrowing. —You sure you know what you're getting into?

She glanced at the resumed game, pretending interest. —I'll need the car, she said, not meeting his eyes. —And don't ask more questions! Playful, a little flirtatious, the way they were when one of them wanted, unaccompanied, to buy a gift for the other. She put a hand out, to soften the abruptness. —You stay here, go to the beach. It doesn't need two of us. Besides, they already know me.

—Don't do anything stupid, he said.

Victoria was on her phone, sitting on her desk among files and papers, glasses pushed up into her curls. —What did you expect? she said when Kate had finished, and then, more kindly: —I know, you want to try. So did we, at the beginning.

Es una tonta, she would probably tell Javier later. *Una caprichosa.* —Look, you want a coffee? I have some news.

Zainab, it turned out, had remembered the name of the boy's village, or so she claimed. She'd told Javier so, at the dinner the evening before. In the bar across the street Victoria ordered two *cafés solos* and sat down. —She will tell only if we take her to ferry to Morocco.

—She's blackmailing us, then.

Victoria tore open a paper tube of sugar, shrugging. —She want to deliver baby there.

—But why? In Zainab's position the last place Kate would have gone was back to Morocco.

—She say is only bad luck here.

—Then why doesn't she go to the police and get deported?

—She thinks they beat her. Or kill her. Last month they are putting man on plane to Tunisia, he dies. Victoria shrugged again, as if such run-of-the-mill tragedy was the way of the world now. Which it probably was.

—The baby'll have Spanish citizenship if she stays, won't it?

A myth, unfortunately, or so Victoria said, though pregnant women arrived every day believing it was true. —Baby will be Moroccan. But Vojtech will help, and others. She is a widow, educated.... Victoria stared out the window, as if already marshalling arguments against an adamantine bureaucracy. —She perhaps have chance. If she tell good story.

—*You're* not going to take her, are you?

—*Claro que no!* Victoria looked horrified. —It is dangerous. For us, of course, but also for her. If she is caught.... She gave Kate a sharp, narrowed stare. —She know we can get whatever we want. Especially you. You would do same thing, no, in her position?

—So she thinks *I'll* help her do this? Kate stared back, thrilled at Zainab's audacity, at what she had seen, or intuited, in Kate.

—She has friend in Casablanca, woman, American woman. Victoria pushed away the half-drunk coffee, frowning. —She say she will go there.

—But if she doesn't have a passport....

—She will find truck, Moroccan truck, going on ferry. Ask driver to hide her. Victoria threw a handful of coins on the table, over Kate's protestations. —You can pay when we learn name of village. If we learn.

She parked beside the large boulder graffitied in Arabic. It had been easy enough to spot and there was a sort of pullout, though she felt exposed, here, in the rental car that advertised her as a visitor. The children came running before she'd turned off the ignition. She handed out a couple of chocolate bars and watched, scandalized, as they fought over them. Two or three older boys stood at a wary distance, smoking.

From the trunk she hauled out the bag of groceries—bread, canned fish, apples—she'd bought before going to the Centro. Those who'd lost out on the chocolate clamoured round her, shoving and pushing. —Can you help, please? she called to the distant boys, but no-one moved. Fortunately here was Nagmeldin, moving down the path with that easy grace.

—I thought you could use—you know. Could hand this out to everyone. Gesturing weakly at the bag that Nagmeldin stooped for and swung to his shoulder. She followed him up the hill, the children swarming. Near the top he glanced round and made a chopping motion, hand held sideways.

—Okay. You go now.

She stopped, stupid with surprise. He hadn't even said thank you. She was a friend, wasn't she?—a friend of friends? The children drifted after him, glancing back with cool indifference. She wasn't leaving, of course—she had a delivery to make. In her daypack were little jars of preserved lemon, Moroccan spices with exotic names—*karfa, skinjbir, tahmira*—that she'd pounced on in the supermarket. An exchange of sorts, though she wouldn't put it like that to Zainab. Nagmeldin might be annoyed, angry even, but he couldn't stop her.

She was almost at the crest when Zainab herself burst out of the bushes above her, panting, clutching a plastic bag to her chest. —You came! You came! She pushed aside a gaping Kate and broke into an awkward run. The children surged downhill again behind them. Zainab, reaching the car, threw herself in and locked the door.

—I can't take you, Zainab, I can't! Kate shouted, arriving seconds too late and seizing the handle.

But Zainab would not get out even when Kate got the door open. The children laughed and gibbered and danced about, enchanted with the absurdity of it all. Kate implored, threatened, grabbed Zainab's arm and pulled. Zainab herself sat in a bubble of calm, looking straight ahead.

—All right. I'll take you as far as the town. Understand?

No response. Kate swore softly under her breath. As she started the car and swerved onto the road the children raced alongside, dropping back into the boil of dust as she gained speed.

—You came, Zainab repeated simply. —All month I pray, all day, every day. And now, *insh'allah*, I will get home.

—You understand, don't you? Kate said when they reached the junction with the main road. —That I'm dropping you in town?

Ahead of them was the highway, glinting with illusory pools of water in the afternoon sun. A car sped past, then one of the inter-village buses on its way into town. Really, it wasn't her problem; it was Zainab's. She'd take Zainab to the Centro and ask them to reason with her. Get her out of the car, at least.

Then she remembered it was Friday. The Centro closed at 1 PM.

—Where were you? Gavin said irritably. He was lying on the bed reading a paperback. Held out his watch, as if she could read it from this distance. —It's almost four.

—I know, I'm sorry, I thought I'd be back. Though she hadn't in fact said so. She kicked a sandal off viciously. —There's a woman in the car.

He rose on an elbow, staring.

—She's from that camp. She wants to go back to Morocco. The hell with it, trying to be careful. —She got in the car and I couldn't get her out. Her voice rose. —Don't ask *questions*, Gavin.

He'd swung his feet to the floor and stood up. She stood up straighter; that way they were even. —She got in the car, he said carefully, slowly. —And what? We're supposed to take her there?

—She won't get out. She's pregnant, Kate added, as if that was a factor in her inability to remove Zainab—which perhaps it was. —I parked two blocks away. She doesn't know where we're staying.

He was staring at her again. —Suppose she's gone to the police to report you? Or that Centro?

It hadn't occurred to her that Zainab might believe she had information she could use.

—She's afraid of them. How dare he criticize her good deed? —Besides, I took some food there.

102

—In our rental car. With easily traceable plates.

Maybe he was jealous. At least she'd *tried*. Taken a risk an earlier Gavin would have applauded, back when he'd talked about working for Doctors Without Borders after medical school. — Why do you care, anyway? she said wildly, incontinently. — You didn't before. Gavin flung the paperback on the bed—he seemed to be making a habit of flinging things—and grabbed his daypack. —We'd better go find her, he said. —Make sure she's okay.

She was where Kate had left her, sitting in the shaded passenger seat, staring straight ahead. Gavin, bending down at the partly opened window, made her startle. He said something that Kate, a short distance away, small and squashable, didn't hear.

—You take me to ferry, please. For the first time Zainab's voice trembled, then solidified. —Only to ferry, nothing more. Please. I am begging.

She was staring up at him, crumpling a corner of her shawl in her hands. They'd trapped him into something, she and Zainab—that must be what he thought. He gave an almost imperceptible shrug. Walked round to the driver's side, body rigid, face held away.

They drove with the windows rolled down, Kate breathing sea air deeply, in and out. Zainab sat with her fingers splayed on her belly, her posture steely. —I am thinking, she announced, out of nowhere, about names. For baby.

What did she think this was, a Sunday drive? —We're taking a big risk, you know, Kate said, her voice shaking. Gavin shot her a warning glance in the rearview.

—Karim if it is boy, Zainab said, as if Kate hadn't spoken. —It means giving, generous. And Abdellatif after my husband. Abdellatif—I don't know in English. Means something like servant of Allah. After a moment she said, as if she was quoting —Danger is like a cheetah. If we show fear it opens its claws.

—We'll drop you, Gavin said (he was carrying on the other conversation, the one they ought to be having), on the outskirts of town. That's safer for all of us. You can make your own way from there.

But Zainab wanted to disappear into crowds somewhere,

103

somewhere no-one would notice. The back of Gavin's neck red-dened, though for once Kate agreed with her. The sun bore down on them, a dagger, striking sparks.

—I am very angry, at first, Zainab said firmly. Angry at the cheetah that had unsheathed its claws? —With Allah, I mean. After what happened to me, to us. Then, you know, I accept. I accept because my husband would say to do.

Kate glanced at her, appalled. She was still obeying her hus-band—she, an educated widow? Zainab laughed, unexpectedly, and threw up her hands. —I find myself on very strange journey. Not here, to Spain—I mean *here*. She pressed a hand to her heart. —I meet my husband at wedding, big family wedding. My fam-ily already has picked out someone, very nice, engineer, good-looking.... Shrugging, as if she found her own behaviour inexplicable. —But then I meet Abdellatif, he is son of my mother's cousin. My family is horrified. He is too young for me, only 22, he is not educated like me at university, he is carpenter, son of a *shaikh*. A teacher of Islam, a Sufi. My father is professor at University of Al-Karaouine, he does not practise religion. Zainab shook her head, as if saddened by her own conduct, or her father's. —I cannot help. I am in love. So we run away, we are married secretly. We are together only a year but I learn a lot from him.

A year. So little time. What did Allah think he was doing, leaving Zainab to fend for herself? —Who knows why? Zainab said, as if answering Kate's question. —But at least I have baby. I hope is boy like his father. But I am happy for girl, too.

—Then why don't you stay here? Gavin said, in his blunt way. —What are you going back for? The road was climbing again, the shot silk of the Mediterranean spread out below them.

—I *hate* here. That air of hostility, flooding the car. —We live, back there, like animals. Lower than animals. Only Victoria and Javier help.

—And me, Kate said quietly.

—Yes, and you. You and your husband. You are my—she pressed her hand to her heart again—my *mala'ikah*. My angels.

Gavin would be rolling his eyes, so she rushed into her ques-tion. —Before you go you must tell me the name of that vil-lage.

Zainab, puzzled, spread her hands. —I do not—

—The boy. That boy from the Rif Mountains—you said—

—Ah yes. She smiled at Kate, turning round to touch her knee. —I think was Bouazzoun. Near Taounate. Or was it Bourdoud? She paused, frowning. —My great-grandfather came from there, long ago. Yes, Bourdoud, I am sure of it now. Tiny place just past Aïn-Aïcha.

They dropped her on a crowded street in the city centre, car horns shrieking behind them. Zainab walked away without looking back, just another Arab woman in a djellaba and head scarf. Why hadn't she asked Zainab the name of the place they'd left from, she and the boy? Unless, of course, she'd simply made it up. Not the village, but the fact of the encounter.

—We can't just abandon her, Gavin said, watching her go. —Suppose the police stop her?

Over Kate's objections they followed at a distance until they lost her, turning down an alleyway. In a café, picking at a sandwich, Gavin was silent, so Kate typed *Bourdoud Morocco* into her phone. Nothing. Too small, probably. The same with *Bouazzoun*. Tiny sunbaked places where old men sat smoking kif.

—We can't go back, Gavin said.

—You mean the hotel?

—Home. Go home without looking for his family. He glared at her, accusatory. —That's what you wanted, isn't it?

They managed to get an evening ferry after a passenger with a reservation failed to show. Gavin went off to wander the decks while Kate stayed in the car. In the next lane a boy in his late teens was staring down at her from the cab of a truck lettered in Arabic. Thin, brown, dark-rimmed eyes—Azemmur himself. He grinned and flickered his tongue, wetting his lips. Made a circle of thumb and forefinger and jabbed the other forefinger through, back and forth.

Not Azemmur after all. Or Azemmur as he might have been, flagrant, strutting. She caught the edge of his teeth as she turned away.

—You need advice, perhaps? Help?

Some blond foreigner in sunglasses and Moroccan shirt had

stopped beside them under the awning of the café. They were drinking *qahwa helib,* café au lait, and trying to wake up; the cries of the muezzins had woken them at 3 AM. He gestured at the map Kate had spread out on the table. Did he know where Bourdoud was, near Âïn-Âïcha?

—You must not go to the Rif, the man said. He was German, or at least German-born; his name was Henk. He had lived in Morocco for 30 years. —The police will arrest you. They will think you are there to buy marijuana. Your story about the boy—he shrugged, drawing down his mouth. —They will not believe you. Men in the Rif do not wear tattoos. Would they like to join him for the best *khobz belbid*—French toast, made with orange juice—in the city?

The restaurant, a ten-minute walk away, stood at the edge of a square with a blue-tiled fountain where men stood or sat in groups, smoking, gesticulating, drinking mint tea. —Here, Henk said softly as they ate, is where you come if you want to leave. Where the fixers find you a way out. He nodded in the direction of Europe. —But it's expensive. Two thousand American dollars at least. Fifteen thousand dirhams. Your boy's family would have pooled their savings, asked relatives. Sold more kif.

Most of the men wouldn't talk, but a younger man about Kate's age, eager to practise English, told them the boy would have left from some empty patch of beach. —Too many coast guard here. Near Fnideq, maybe. Or Oued Laou. He shrugged. —Everyone knows the risks. But to die once is better than dying ten times in the face of your parents' pity.

Oued Laou was only 60 kilometres away but a two-hour drive at least because of road construction. They set out in the car, the three of them, in the stinking heat, Henk having offered to come along as translator and guide. Suicidal motorbikes, their riders' shirts flapping behind them, zipped in and out. A donkey plodded past in the dust, laden with electric fans. Across the Alborán Sea Spain shimmered dizzily.

Henk was vague about what he did. People hired him to make maquettes, designs, that sort of thing—enough to live well in Moroccan terms. He was 54. In Germany there was nothing left for him. What kept him here? The intensity, the way people lived every moment as if it was their last. He pointed out the window, naming trees, birds, even dust-covered weeds. Germany lived, still, under the shadow of the war his father had fought in, on the wrong side.

On the edge of town, almost four hours later, they were directed to a wooden doorway and a man in a shabby brown suit, slender and wary, who sat drinking coffee. Yes, he could get someone to Spain, for the right price, though he shook his head at the tattoo. *Milles des personnes*, he said wearily, translating into Spanish for good measure. He couldn't possibly remember them all. Yes, some of them died, but that was their fate, or the fault of the boat owners. He was simply supplying a service. No, he didn't want to go himself. The Spaniards had thrown them out, centuries ago, though the Arabs had given them everything—mathematics, running water, the names of stars. There was gratitude for you!

Gavin, over lamb tagine and wine, argued for going back. — We're not getting anywhere. If we leave now we might make an evening ferry.

—But we've only just started. Haven't we, Henk? We're not even in the Rif yet.

—Excuse us, Gavin said, rudely, before Henk could answer, and walked Kate outside. —Kate. Katie. He took her hands in his. —I know you want to help, and it's wonderful of you. I know I said we should come. But it's pointless, what we're doing, don't you see?

So it had all been a ruse, their coming. She would see how silly it was and then they'd go back to their holiday. They would pretend, just like Zainab.

—He chose me, she said simply. —Your science doesn't explain everything, does it. He's relying on me.

They argued all night in their room in the only pension in Fnideq, which was where, for no good reason, they ended up. —I'm at your service, Henk had told them, if Kate wants to go on. I'm free at the moment. No ulterior motives, he added, and flung up his hands as if they'd pointed a gun at him.

With Henk as her guide she'd be quite safe, Kate said. Gavin, explosive: It wasn't about Henk, it had nothing to do with

Henk! —Take the car, she said. —Leave early. Maybe you'll make the ferry before the roadwork starts. At dawn, before he left, he touched her face with his fingers while she pretended sleep.

She and Henk waited two hours for the bus that would take them into the mountains. When it came it bore men with roped bundles, the odd djellaba'ed woman, half-a-dozen live chickens. Among a handful of houses that might have been a village, Henk indicated they should get off. —You must look as if you belong to a man, he said, and took her arm as if they were a couple.

Kate's drawing was passed from hand to hand among the old men who gathered, frowning under their headwraps. —They're telling us what we already know, Henk explained. —That it's a tattoo, what it means. Though they say it's not accurate. Women brought plates of *kefta* and couscous, eyeing Kate openly, faces sharp with disapproval.

The next village involved a battered taxi and a rock-strewn, lurching drive. An ancient woman, evidently deaf, stared at them in astonishment while several children peered from a doorway. No-one else seemed to be about. Henk took off his hat and mopped his face. To Kate's relief a boy appeared, leading a donkey. Everyone was away at some religious festival, he told Henk, who arranged to hire the donkey to carry them, or rather her, along an uphill goat track to the next village. They arrived as the sun was setting. Another handful of buildings that seemed to have assembled themselves out of the arid pastures—she'd never seen life so stripped to its basics. The place glowed with evening light; a bat flapped past her head. They were offered a couple of mattresses in one of the houses, where a middle-aged woman with the grave face of a saint brought them some sort of bean soup and bread to scoop it up with. Afterwards she took a blanket and lay outside watching the stars, in their brilliant indifference, come out, one by one.

In the fifth—or was it the sixth?—village, a young woman appeared who knew some English. She seemed to emerge from a group of chattering children and offered Kate a glass of what turned out to be fresh lemonade. Together with an older woman she guided Kate into the dimness of a shuttered room with a low bed, where she must have slept because the sun was setting when she woke. She made her way, groggily, toward the voices outside.

—So you found a body, the young woman said, arms folded, leaning against the doorway of the house as Kate sat eating the food she'd brought. She wore jeans and nailpolish along with her head scarf. —You came all this way because you found a body?

Kate, mouth full of couscous, nodded, though with the food warming her belly she'd half-forgotten Azemmur. The young woman produced a cigarette, lit it, blew out smoke. Her own brother had gone missing in Spain seven years before. He was the oldest, he was expected to provide for his parents and younger siblings. Her father believed he'd taken up with a foreign girl and was keeping all his money for himself. Had denounced him, publicly, announcing that his son was no longer his son, that in fact he'd never existed.

—So I went to Fez to look for work, after we didn't hear from him. I was lucky, I knew some English, I got a job in a hotel.

Now it was her younger brother who wanted out. He was only fifteen but he'd probably go to Spain next year, or the year after that. He came up as she spoke, a startlingly handsome boy with long eyelashes and a shy smile. Said something to his sister, whose name, apparently, was Lalla. She frowned and flicked her fingers at him and muttered something.

—It is time for our English lesson, she told Kate. —He is always saying English, English. Perhaps I am helping him drown, too. But what choice did they have? —Even the goats here have nothing to eat, with the drought, she said. She swept her arm across the hillside and gave Kate a look of undisguised envy. — You know any man in Morocco would marry you in an instant, don't you? Just like that—she snapped her fingers. —And here *you* are, looking for a man who doesn't even belong to you.

In the evening Lalla took her from house to house. In each she held out the drawing, now smudged and torn from so much handling. In each the answer was the same. No, they knew of no such boy. It was doubtful, indeed, that such a boy existed, one whose mother would have him tattooed like that. What boy would agree to such a thing? What father? Not for the first time Kate wondered about Zainab's explanation, the one she said the boy himself had given. Perhaps, like the boy's home village, that too was made up. Instead they told her about their own sons, the ones they'd lost to that narrow strait that separated Morocco from the continent. They held out photographs, they cried names aloud, they called on Allah as witness. In the last house a middle-aged woman who must once have been a beauty took a framed photograph from its place in an alcove surrounded by candles, kissed it, then held it out to Kate. A child still, the boy in the photograph, with his downy face and dreamy eyes. He'd left when he was sixteen, the woman said as Lalla translated. — He's 37 now, if he's still alive, *insh'allah*. Here, take, you take. And she thrust the photo into Kate's hands, refusing to take it back. —Look for this boy instead. He's still alive, I'm sure of it. I have a little money, I can pay. And she fumbled coins from her kaftan, though Kate held her hands behind her back. It was Lalla who intervened, who handed the photo back to the woman and said to Kate —Don't you dare take him on. Go home. Find your husband.

She vomited up the meal that Lalla and her mother prepared the next morning, couldn't even keep water down. In the cool room where the shutters were drawn, Lalla's mother bathed her forehead and hands with rosewater and left her to rest. She dozed from time to time, jerking out of sleep. She would search until he told her to stop. She'd met his family, after all, in these little villages—his sisters and brothers, his aunts, his grandparents. She'd eaten their food, slept on their mattresses of straw. They asked their god to bless her journey, they urged her to let them know if she found the boy's family. He had left, like all the others, for an unknown country, one with no passports, no immigration controls, an underwater country populated by the dead. They lay among the waving seaweed, the fat darting fish.

Toward evening Azemmur came. He was bathed in a kind of shining radiance. He lit a candle that seemed to be floating on a bowl of fragrant oil. —I am grateful, *khtî*, he told her gently, but you will not find me. He turned, then, smiling, and walked toward the ocean she hadn't noticed until now. She wept and pleaded but he moved resolutely on. She sat down on the sand, cold and shaking, and watched him until his head disappeared beneath the waves.

She woke to voices—Henk and someone else—discussing something in hushed tones. Someone, a woman she had never seen before, came in and held a concoction of bitter herbs to her lips. Perhaps she was dying, though she didn't think so. She had been granted a glimpse across a border, that was all. Gavin had seen the Alhambra and the village where the Moors fought the Christians, but the place she had seen was in no guidebook that she knew of. Azemmur had led the way, and she had followed. A tiny bit of radiance lingered just below the shutters, where the ocean had seeped in.

The Fires of Soweto
Heather Davidson

Chickens pecked around his feet, the house behind him risen alien out of the veld's landscape. Inside, they drank murky rooibos tea when what he really wanted was the slap of fresh coffee. His wife Jodi had collarbones visible below her neck like he had never noticed them before, her man's button-down shirt open over a white cotton tank-top and ivory pendant necklace on a leather cord. Braiding her long hair over her shoulder as she spoke to him, cross-legged on a chair. She sat far away from him at the table, ate as her parents did with their elbows beside the plate, leaning forward to gesture with bread in their hands.

And she expected him to follow her, to be as familiar as she was with the property and the names of the men who worked around it. "That's Prosper," she said after the meal, pointing at a man in blue coveralls. Then she turned on the outside tap to fill a dish with water for the Rhodesian Ridgeback, Wally. She wore shorts and rubber boots, and he watched the peaks of her shoulder blades appear from underneath her oversized shirt. He had nothing to do except wait for the party her parents, the Pieks, were hosting that night, get through it and then drive with Jodi to the airport the next afternoon.

Her thinness was just the latest incarnation of disease, making her look especially vulnerable against the desert-wash colours of South Africa. He had been calling his wife's illness 'the cancer' for so long, refusing to think of it in specifics or recognize it by speaking its name. And she was the opposite, mapping out with an eerie and horrified fascination the details of her failing organs. It was at the party when they first fought about it, the two of them ringing the kitchen in their stranded way, while he watched her peel plastic wrap back from a silver tray of brownies. "Jodi," he whispered, "you don't need to tell them about all your symptoms. They don't need to know about the sweats and the puking. It's okay. No-one will doubt you if you just say that you're not well." He regretted that she would take it as accusatory, because he had no better way to say it.

She sighed; looking back at the lights of the full table like it was a city in the distance. "No-one cares as much as you do," she said; quiet, sliding the tray off the counter. And she walked out, back into the dining-room, and he realised that instead of words there was only silence dying in his throat. He sat through the desserts and coffee afraid that with every detail he was exposed in his failings as a caregiver. She looked at him over her mug and then looked away. He wanted to tell her that pain shared was not always lessened, that too much sharing would only mean giving others the means to harm you in the future.

She found him outside later, smoking, miserable, and trying to follow the shape of Prosper or someone else as he walked by with firewood. But the darkness was so complete that he felt it as a secrecy he was not part of, a loss that had taken from him even the outlines of the fences. She was angry with someone, he could tell, and he waited to see if she was going to tell him what it was about. And she did, pulling each strap of her lavender dress back toward her neck, with the same one finger. "He's dumb as an ox sometimes, my father," she finally said. Martin Piek wore horn-rimmed glasses and liked to light his pipe in a rocking chair on the porch of the house. Sitting with his tan legs crossed, in shorts, canvas shoes, and a zip-up sweater.

"Maybe he is. But we do have feelings. Men, I mean. Surprisingly." She looked at his cigarette then with such interest that he was tempted to give her one, but he didn't. "So what are you going to do now?"

She bent to pull her shoe off, sliding the strap across a patch of chafed red skin on her heel. When Jodi straightened, it was with some new calm. "I'm going driving." She had started to turn away. "You should come."

Even with the headlights on, he had no idea where they were going or how she could navigate. But she stopped the jeep, and then he noticed the small fire off to the left side. "It's just the watchman," she said, tilting her seat back. The night seemed to hum with a sense of aliveness that he had never felt even in New York. The fire smoked and crackled. Was she drunk? He could smell something on her, maybe the same cheap musky cologne her father wore, and which she liked to borrow. He could not find a sense of time in this dark.

"Did you know," he said, "that your cousin told me you can see all the cooking fires in Soweto and the townships when you fly into Jo'burg at night?"

She said nothing for one long sweet breath. "You shouldn't judge me like you're doing. I hate them sometimes and I escaped them, but I need them right now. And I talk in clinical details because that's all they can handle. We drink together and I never say I'm scared and they never say they love me."

He flattened into the seat back, gripping the doorframe. "It's...it's a funny way your family has of dealing with bad news. Your uncle Christian getting murdered by a burglar and they almost seemed to think it was his fault."

She sighed. "Yes, we're very sad about that. But it's true, he should have known better. There's a, you know, way to react to robbers around here and he didn't follow it. Maybe I'm a hypocrite. But cancer isn't a boy with a gun, and there's no procedure to follow so you'll get out alive."

No, cancer is a bush dog that steals your chickens and then begins eyeing you through the window at night, he thought. A foe who may want more than you can replace. He was frightened at the kind of wildness she came from, she whom he called his unflappable girl. They sat silent and then with paced movements he moved slowly toward her. She flopped like a miserable child, cheek against his armpit. Lifting slightly to aid him as he smoothed the dress down. A cold gasp of night air came through a crack in the left window. And the silk dress slid away from him but at least she didn't, because he was just a man after all and right now he needed something tangible to hold onto.

She had taken up smoking just recently, after coming back to New York, when she saw the package of cigarettes in her husband Garrett's coat pocket and slid one out. It surprised her, how easy it was to inhale and exhale, how it felt languorous even. In the patch of scrub behind their apartment building, she sat on the grass with her little burning ember, listening to the sounds from the hidden street out front, the cars from the bridge. The thwack, thwack of a child's skipping rope hit like a stick striking the flanks of pupils she used to see bent over in the schoolyard, when they drove from the farm into Cape Town. Women in aprons and headwraps bringing laundry out to hang, with their naked babies running around, only T-shirts to cover the tops of their bellies. She thought of what the children called when they saw her arm out the window of the jeep. *White lady, white lady*, though she was only eleven or twelve. Now getting dirt smeared onto her skin when she lay back to rest against a concrete stub, remembering. How she studied apartheid and protested and lost friends because she heard a bright cold music when they told her lies about race. *But white lady can't turn brown.*

It was spring in Brooklyn, when the weeds were harsh and stubbly against the pavement but existent nonetheless. A few days after their week-long trip to South Africa and she was un-moored, still on leave from work at the women's shelter and sup-posed to occupy herself while she waited to start chemotherapy. She was waiting for Garrett as well, waiting for him to come and find her when he got home from the university, for his re-action when he smelled the smoke on her clothes. Maybe she could light another one, show him how well she did it. She had only started coughing toward the end, when she crushed the butt and stuck it in her pocket. And then he did finally come, and she called out to the slice of him visible past the corner.

"What are you doing, lovely?" He pulled the long strap of his laptop bag over his head; let it down at his feet. She fingered a loose bootlace of his, and he bent to kiss her forehead. He did smell the cigarette, she could tell as he sat down beside her. Nos-trils drawn back and out, asking, "Where did you pick that up from?" She laughed, taking the water bottle from his bag's holder for a swig.

"I just wanted to experiment with smoking. Figure I've earned the right to a new vice." He had the surprise and quick acceptance that she associated with a native New Yorker, dragged with what seemed like willingness to Jodi's choice of the Lower East Side, then Williamsburg. He paused, started to rise, and she thought that he must really want to go inside, relax, adjust from his work to home life.

"Hey, I have an idea. Let's go up on the fire escape." He lifted himself onto the black rungs, pulling her after him. They dangled their feet over the side, felt the breeze as it fingered its way through the railings.

Just then he was thinking of what New York used to be like for him, running up and down the stairs of fire escapes on buildings that should have been condemned, how he hung his laundry over the shower curtain rod, the time his roommates and he smoked meat on the roof and the smoke blew into the sky like the apartments were on fire. All that red brick, the strike of a match against boot-heels.

And they had marked the changing seasons with the fervour of pagans. Winter was the name of a girl who left them, covered herself up with leaves. And spring this year found him, at 43 years old, a photographer and university professor. Sitting with his South African-born wife below a sky that was the lightest blue of the button-down shirt she wore.

"Do you want to drive out to Montauk this weekend?" He realised that he longed for the loom motion of the waves. All his photos that month had been of city landscapes, buildings that looked as if they were climbing all over each over. A change was needed, and maybe he should spend some peaceful time with her, now that she was turning to cigarettes. Another surprise, and he had thought there were none of those left.

"Sure, that could be fun." She flicked a leaf off into the grass. "Don't worry so much about the smoking, Gar. It's just hard to think that I'm going to have to be so damn healthy from now on. Imagine the sixties, any other time like that when they smoked and drank the same as breathing. God, what did we do before we knew everything that could kill us?"

She loved him for the seriousness that overtook his face, when his eyes were so wide open that they seemed to need his cheekbones to support them. When he looked at her. So she kept speaking, said, "The last time we had to drive out that far...at the faculty barbeque, I lost you, I was going crazy. And remember where you were when I found you? In the basement, looking at a broken projector." Scratching at the dirt with a fingernail, feeling it cool against her skin. "You've always wanted to be useful." It had the warm-egg feeling of a realisation. His neck in the softening light was the white grace of a teapot handle, a vase's curve. "You need a shave," she said, soft into his ear. And he pressed his stubbly chin into her cheek until she laughed, pushing him away by the shoulder. But not too far away.

She stood in the living-room the next morning, where she wore their white cat Milk like a boa over her shoulders with his tail along her spine, brushing against the ladder of bone. Thinking about the things that she wished she could say to the black teenage boys who sneered at her from outside convenience stores. Their voices, like the sounds of traffic, had a frantic rhythm. There was always a car horn or an ambulance siren to be startled by when she and Garrett were in bed and trying to be so slow and unhurried. Or maybe it was only she who thought like that, since he did not remember it when she told it to him. "Languid love," he joked, "and then we went back to tending our vineyards." True, he was forever in a rush, riding his bike back home with fresh rolls from the bakery as she carried a book and a blanket outside. And now she could tell that he had fantasies of taking her away to the country where it would be quiet and he could do things like chop wood and make soup. A change of direction, but the same energy. It might be possible to blame her torpor on her being African, she thought. Even sick and possibly dying, we take our time.

She felt the new bareness of her neck, her hands still surprised at how much less of her hair there was to comb through. Garrett always looked so vulnerable after a fresh haircut, pale scalp and maybe a tiny nick behind his ear. Better to start cutting her hair gradually, so it would be less of a shock, the oncology nurses told her. She set the cat down and walked toward the bedroom. The doctor's appointment was in an hour, and she thought of how much time she could take from that hour before leaving. Make tea, walk the dog if she had the energy. Banjo was sprawled against the kitchen cupboards, his head angled to watch the door for movement. But at the closet she knew it would be best to just leave. Pulling on a loose, drapy sweater, because it felt like protection the way the knit fabric hid her exact contours. She felt like she needed to be dressed in some proper way, even just speaking to a nurse on the phone, as if they would be able to tell what she was wearing. That was what being an adult meant, she thought. Taking the time to do all these little things that nobody notices or cares about, but that still matter somehow.

Garrett sat at the table in the middle of the kitchen, gauging the minutes before he had to leave for the school. And no wonder he was touching the surface of it somehow, leaning on it with hips and hands. Because the rest of the world seemed to be floating away. When she left for an appointment he was never sure what to do. He thought about her in bed that morning, how it was so much white for him to look at, her skin blending in with the sheets and comforter and the labels on pill bottles. Her cotton bra and underwear because she sweated too much in pyjamas, and one small hand resting up above the pillow. He remembered how, back in January, she lost one of her mittens during a subway transfer and they only noticed once in the aboveground world again. "It's all right," she said, "it just means that you have to hold my hand from now on." She had made a small fist inside his grasp, and the wind marked both of their skins.

He was going to call her phone, leave a message if she was already in the hospital and couldn't answer. Yet it was almost independent of his arm, the way his hand and fingers coordinated to pick up the phone from its cradle. Why so difficult? He needed to ask how she felt, but was afraid to know—what if she felt terrible? Maybe nothing he could do to change that. Busy man, work as usual, full lecture hall of students for *Intro to the History of Photography*. And yet he was lucky because he could say that being with Jodi yesterday afternoon had been the type of moment when what you want and what you have meet, and you realise they are the same thing. Maybe he wouldn't be able to express everything in one conversation, but he was determined to do better than just ask for the latest medication she had been prescribed. Because worrying about her he felt as empty as a clean-swept hallway. Strange that your love for someone could empty you out like that, make you need to be filled up in return. And so he picked up the phone.

You Know How I Feel
Elisabeth de Mariaffi

Ruby refuses to sleep until after Sudbury. I want to be buried in suds, she says. I want a bubble bath in Sud-Buried.

It's six hours in the car and they don't even stop. Gas, once. The car's a rental, small and zippy and silver. Great pick-up: what the rent-a-car man said, handing over the keys. You get out on the highway and give 'er. There's a bounce to the gearshift, or Sarah bounces it. Out on the highway she gives 'er, and they stay in fifth for three hours straight. They left at five in the morning so Ruby would sleep.

Sarah doesn't have a car seat for her. Why should she? They never take a car in the city. And Ruby's got to be 40 pounds by now or close to it, and anyway, didn't we all ride across the country without car seats in the seventies?

Glenna will be horrified.

Glenna will be charmed by this and tell and retell the story at dinner that night. Silas, pick that child up and tell me she's 40 pounds. Sarah, we will *give* you a car seat, we'll give it to you. We must have an old one around here somewhere.

How many at dinner. Sarah and Ruby. Glenna, Silas, their three boys, her two parents. Plus plus plus. Some assortment of others, friends or almost-cousins or whoever else Glenna can pull in for a week away. Drunk Silas, his arm snaked around Sarah's waist, hand under her clothes. The same the last two summers: Sarah changing into pyjamas in the safety of her locked car, Silas wandering the lawn at two in the morning. Ruby asleep, waiting for Sarah in the tent.

We're very lucky, Sarah says out loud. We get a whole bunkhouse to ourselves. Like a cabin. Like a fort, she says.

How about we sleep in a tent? Ruby says.

No, Sarah says. A bunkhouse. A little house for just us. She flicks her eyes up to the rearview. But we can put a special net over your bed to keep the mosquitoes away.

Like a tent? Ruby says.

Like a canopy, Sarah says. Like a princess.

She sprays some wiper fluid and sets the arms going on the windshield. Ruby closes her eyes and tips down toward the bench in the backseat.

In Sud-Buried I will have a creamy bath of round, pink bubbles, she says. And a princess bed with a beautiful lace tent.

Silas is out in the gravel drive when they pull in, smoking a joint where Glenna can't see him. Bent over a bike tire to make it look like he's doing something. Watching, Sarah thinks, for this car. For Sarah and Ruby.

Beckett!

He pinches the roach tight between his fingers, slides it into the breast pocket of his shirt. A strong, fast hug, his arms wrapped firm around her back and then gone. Sarah springs the hatch and starts hauling gear out onto the ground: duffle bags, the cooler, a sleeping bag in case they need it. Silas pops the passenger door.

Hey Ruby-Ruby! Pushes a finally sleepy Ruby along toward the cottage and comes back for Sarah.

Took you long enough, Beckett.

Sarah points to the sleeping bag. Silas shakes his head and she throws it back in the car and slams the door.

I forgot you're a betting man, she says. I hate to disappoint. I had $40 on you at 10:30.

Five-year-old in the back, remember.

Five, shmive, Silas says. You've cost me. How about a drink. Is it noon?

Different rules up here, my friend.

How many, Sarah says, meaning rules or guests, whatever Silas comes up with first.

Let's see. Silas half-shuts one eye in the manner of the thinking man. There's us and you. That's seven, if you include children. Do we?

Yes.

All right then. Seven. Glenna's parents. Nine. Mike and Ilsa. You met them once in the city.

He never talks, Sarah says. Why doesn't he ever talk?

He's a mute, of course. All the best men are. Silas pauses. They have a baby now, it's awful, you can't stand it, don't talk to Ilsa if you can help it. So what's that?

Twelve, Sarah says.

With children.

Yes, with.

Seven without, Silas says.

But we get the bunkhouse still, Sarah says. Me and Ruby, that hasn't changed. She leans down and takes a bag in each hand.

Is that a good thing?

It's good. It's good for Ruby, Sarah says. Of course it means I can't even jerk off by myself.

If only you'd learn to keep your mouth shut, Silas says.

The screen door slaps shut and Glenna is outside, her blonde hair pulled back smooth and clean, wearing a blue one-piece, Sarah can see, under her dress.

Sarah, Glenna says.

She holds Sarah by the elbows.

At dinner Silas announces: Beckett's a poet!

The others at table shift in their seats. What now?

Glenna: We all know her, Silas.

Not Mike and Ilsa. Mike, did you know Beckett writes poems? Books and everything.

Ilsa, Sarah says to distract from the unsettling business of her own poem-writing. The bottle stands by you.

Ilsa is short and pretty, with red hair tied up in a knot of bobby pins. She's round in a way that Sarah admires. Imagine being round like that, Sarah thinks. Imagine that belly. She perceives fat women not as happy, exactly, but perhaps blithe. Free of doubt. The blanket of flesh between their hips also insulating against too much thinking.

Sarah pours and Silas pouts at his end of the table. Oh come on, Beckett.

I haven't got any stories.

Men.

There haven't been any, Sarah says. I'm shamefully celibate. I went out with one, for dinner. He was married. I was almost sure he was married when he asked me. I went so I could prove it to myself.

Do you know when I met Beckett? Silas turns to Mike, who twitches with alarm at the attention. Have I told this story? New Year's Eve. He looks wildly around, suddenly discovering Sarah again. You had that crazy house with all the stairs. Ruby was only toddling.

Sarah nods at her own glass. She was in diapers.

Oh, I don't know, Silas says. Glenna, where were you. Why was I there alone.

I went home, Glenna says.

Right, Silas says. His shirt cuffs are unbuttoned and the flapping sleeves give him the look of a fallen duke—as if the estate could be seized at any time. I meant to go, too, he says, but it was blackout time and, and everything went dark kind of. I come to, and I'm on this white, white couch in a white living-room. I thought, Is this the mental ward or what, but when I looked around and saw all the things, you know, the accessories, they were so nice.

Glenna lays a hand flat on the table: Silas. That's enough.

So I wake up and I hear some girl and guy just beating the shit out of each other you know? That was Beckett and Marcus. Right, Beckett? But she didn't seem like one of those ladies tied to the tracks, I didn't have to rescue her. So I ostriched it. Like this, I went back to sleep. Silas folds his hands into a pillow and settles down for a moment next to his dinner plate, then bobs back up. She was giving good as she got, he says. And I wake up a few hours later with some little blondie bouncing around on me. Happy New Year! Happy New Year! That was Ruby. And I sat up, Hello, and there were all these people around I didn't know and here's Beckett: lalala! mojitos! shrimp ring! Silas pushes his hair back with one hand and grips the table-edge with the other, holding himself down.

I ended up staying for two days, he says. Beckett wouldn't let me go! I stayed for two days eating fucking shrimp ring.

Two days, Glenna says, wine glass in hand. And Sarah was the one who got a divorce.

So you're co-parenting. Ilsa turns to Sarah. That's good. I mean, you have your independence. The grass is always greener, right?

It's like being a homeless person, Sarah says. You never know where your next meal is coming from.

Silas: What are you talking about down there, Beckett. Are you talking about fucking.

In my next marriage, Glenna says, I think I'll be the reckless one.

Mike gives Ilsa a hard look.

Sarah turns to Glenna. Where's Ruby? Is she in bed?

Glenna's mother took Ruby for a pedal boat in the afternoon. A kind of pity. People are always wanting Sarah to take time off. As if parenting were some new and difficult task when really it has always been just her and Ruby.

We're all done with kids! Silas says to the room and his sleeve catches the rim of a glass, sending a spray of shiraz across the tablecloth.

Salt! Glenna jumps up.

White wine! Silas yells and grabs for Mike's glass.

Sarah's own glass is empty again. To Ilsa she says, He was away, working on a play. Anyway he was away a lot.

I shot my guns in the air for a while, Sarah says.

The men start stacking dishes, apart from Silas who leans on one hand.

Are a lot of them married?

Shocking, Sarah says. Isn't it.

It's not, Ilsa says. Take a look at you. Men always think they're entitled, but really. I fetishize your breasts. I secretly love your breasts.

Mike, in the kitchen with dishes, takes on a look of resignation.

You don't seem to be afraid of any of it, Ilsa says.

Glenna's mother calls from outdoors: Someone's baby's crying! But it's a loon, they realize it as soon as Ilsa has run from the room.

In the morning there are cheese omelettes. Sarah shows Ruby how to wash her feet in the water bucket by the door. There's a bucket by every door, she says. No sandy toes in the house, okay?

She pulls a kayak down into the water. Silas on the dock, plate in hand, heels together. His back to her: a kind of lameness in the way he stands. He's softened in the way married men do, men who feel somewhat guaranteed. Sarah with her notebook in a zippered plastic bag in case of a spill. She wades out to the knees and climbs in, gripping the bag between her thighs, and paddles quickly. It's a small lake and she wants to be out in it, far enough to blur anything familiar, the children shrieking at their dock wars. She'd woken early and boiled water for coffee, watched Glenna's parents steal a kiss in the lean-to, the old man stuffing a pipe with tobacco. Honey, they called each other. Sarah watching, rubbing the tender insides of her wrists together in the kitchen window.

She comes around an outcrop of rock and pine, Crown land, thick with brush, and into the bay. Sets the paddle carefully across the open seat of the kayak and pulls the notebook out from between her legs. It's hot and still on the water. She tugs the brim of her straw hat down lower around her face. High up, there are white clouds moving fast: now sunny, now shade. Now sun again.

Marcus when they were first together, blond hair falling over his eyes, dancing wild around her room. The back of his T-shirt a wet V. What Mozart would look like, Sarah said, if he were born in 1971. Washing dishes in Sarah's sink wearing her pink rubber gloves. Sarah naked in the kitchen, poaching eggs, beating the linoleum with her red patent heels. At night they ran down the stairs and traced thick chalk outlines of themselves beneath the balcony, waited up until morning to see the look on the Italian Nonna who lived next door and watered her tubs of plastic roses until mould curled around the edges of the leaves. In bed Sarah held a pen and tried to work while Marcus twined her hair around his fingers and ran his hand along her ribcage and squeezed at her nipples underneath her shirt and nudged her thighs apart with his own knee and took away the book and slapped at the pen and slid his hands beneath her hips and stroked into her cleanly twice and three times and then stopped until she asked him and asked him again to please, please make her come.

The kayak smacks up against something and Sarah grabs at the paddle. It's shady and cool. She looks down and there are rocks. Shallows. The brim of the hat pulled so low that she didn't see how far she'd drifted, aground, cool not because of clouds, but because of shade, the cast of trees above her.

She wedges the book back between her knees and pushes off firmly with the paddle, kayak scraping the stony lake floor, then out of the bay and toward open water. Her shoulders stiff with sun. Sitting up taller, she pushes the paddle deep, twirling it on every stroke until she's moving swift and clean. This brings the wind up, or the feel of it. Where is Ruby. Sarah can't see her from this bend. Someone has her, certainly, has given her a sensible lunch. She slacks off and listens to her breath, hard and fast. The paddle crossways, resting lightly in the crease between thumbs and forefingers.

There's a cry and Sarah sees the loon. It's the male, twenty feet to the right of her. Then only ten. Close. Does he know she's a boat. He dips under the surface and Sarah counts, but he doesn't come up. Then she sees him, around the other side of the kayak. Maybe three or four minutes under water. He lets a cry loose over the lake and the echo rings back, the sound like another bird calling. Tucked in an inlet, the female is quiet, busy with her babies. Fish in mouth, he calls again, twitches in the direction of the echo.

You're not calling to her at all, Sarah says out loud.

She dips the paddle and moves closer.

That loon killed a beaver this time last year, Glenna says.

She's out on the dock as Sarah paddles in, page-turner in hand, creamy layer of sunscreen not quite soaked into the skin on her thighs. He came up from underneath. Their beaks are like scissors, you know. Beaver shot straight up into the air. People saw it across the bay.

I seemed to make him nervous, Sarah says. She hauls the kayak up where the dirt is dry-baked, flips it so the bottom-side glints in the sun. It's not a heavy boat, but it catches in the long grass. Sarah's shoulders and thin spine showing as she tugs it into place, her slim legs curving out from the bottom of her bathing suit.

He just doesn't want you close to his family, that's all, Glenna says.

Where's Ruby?

She's on ride-along. My dad took her to the dump. I think she's hoping to catch a bear. Glenna sets the book down and raises a hand to shade her eyes. He's been feeding her stories about how we live in the Bear Capital of the World.

Did she eat? Sarah picks up the tube of sunscreen and squirts a sausage of white into her hand, rubs this into her belly and under the band of her bikini top, then around the back of her neck.

We made sandwiches. Jesus there's nothing on you, is there?

It's an optical illusion, Sarah says. I'm heavier than I look. She sets the cream back on the table and falls into a chair. Was I gone long? I'm working something up in my head, sometimes I lose track of time.

We've got Ruby. Glenna pulls her feet and ankles onto the chair and sits curled up. You mean working like writing-working.

Like that, yes.

I was worried you were upset, Glenna says. Because of Silas, you know. He should keep his stories to himself. Her ankles are crossed. Sarah can see the first hint of sunburn on her breastbone, the skin ruddy and loose-looking.

Oh, about Marcus, she says. Sarah takes off the hat and shakes her hair out. It's all right. It's what happened, right? I used to say if it were high school, I'd have broken up with Marcus a thousand times.

Glenna tilts her head a moment.

I look at you and Silas, Sarah says. Do you think I'll ever get my shit together.

Silas gets drunk, Glenna says. It's his fatal flaw. I look across the room and see him dancing sexy with some girl and I just go home.

Why don't you dance, Sarah says. If he wants to.

He only thinks it's what he wants.

Sarah looks down at her sprawling legs. Something about

Glenna makes her feel gangly, pubescent, too naked.

I wish I'd left Marcus years ago, she says.

From the other side of the house there's a motor, there are tires on gravel, voices.

You know what I think? Glenna stands up and wraps a towel around her waist. All of us, we all do the things we really want to. I believe that. So all that wishful talk, I wish you'd do this or that, I wish I'd married the kind of girl that will dance with me: it's just a way of excusing our own bad behaviour. It's the same with regret.

Sarah squints up. Glenna bends from the waist, gripping the towel with one hand, picks up her book.

Is that Ruby? Sarah says.

We've got Ruby, Glenna says. You just take care of yourself.

Sarah sits out on the dock a while longer, until the wind comes up and it's too cold to pretend to work anymore, even with her jeans pulled on over top of the bikini. She goes and lies down on the bed and her knees drop open. Unzips. Ruby is safely away.

She gets her hand going. It's not Marcus she thinks of, not anymore, not for a long time, but a kind of faceless stand-in. Blond still, but with a beard. Spare and muscled. A vein running down his forearm.

Whose cunt is it? Yours baby. Whose tits? Yours. Who owns you? You do, baby, you do. It's all for you, now let me come, please....

Through the particle board she can hear Mike and Ilsa, the baby crying.

When's it look like for dinner?

They're aiming at seven.

You can hear the clinking plates and that, so I guess it'll be soon. Smells amazing. We could smell it out on the lake.

Take it, Sarah thinks, *take it*.

In the evening they take the children fishing: just Sarah and Silas. The rowboat loaded with rods, Ruby and the three boys, Sarah showing Ruby how to bisect a worm with her sharp fingernail and hook just a piece.

They're wiggling! Ruby squeals and pinches her own worm

into two halves. All the pieces keep wiggling!

Glenna stays on the dock with her book, the others talking about a bonfire or cards. Glenna's mother with her long white hair twisted up and pinned at the neck, on the shore picking sticks, things to burn in the fire. Honey, she calls out, and the old man answers from the lean-to where he's got Glenna's bicycle up on a rack, fitting a new tube into the tire.

I'm sorry I told that story last night. Silas presses the rod handle, ready-cast, into Ruby's hand. Looks up at Sarah. About New Year's Eve. It wasn't fair.

Glenna?

Wouldn't fuck me because of it. He grins down into the styrofoam bait bucket. The youngest boy's small hand in there, massaging many worms at once.

You made it sound so simple, Sarah says. The way men fight. Easy. With a drink to follow-up.

That's how it seemed at the time.

At the time you were half-dead with bourbon.

Silas casts his own line, the hook sailing out and falling precisely, a tiny anchor. You never seem like someone who needs taking care of.

I wish we had scissors, Sarah says to Ruby, who has lost her bait, possibly on purpose.

Why? Ruby says, pinching.

Sarah turns back to Silas. It always surprised me, you know. Every time. Because we had fights, lots of fights, that stopped with screaming. She forces the worm onto Ruby's hook, throws her wrist and hands the line back: Now pull it in nice and slow. The fish need to see your worm swimming along.

Minding his own business, Ruby says.

He was a strong enough guy for his size, Silas says.

Men are, Sarah says.

It probably would have been much worse if you hadn't fought back.

Well I did, Sarah says. I mean, you stop fighting when you don't care. She straightens her back and leans out. What's that?

What's what?

Here. There's something in the water.

You'll tip the boat.

I won't. You lean the other way. It's a rod. Sarah throws a quick glance over the children. Did we lose a rod? She dips a hand into the water and grabs a blue fishing rod out by the handle. There's a long line on it and she reels in quickly, pulling in a shining, slapping bass, sixteen or seventeen inches.

Mommy! Ruby drops her own rod in her lap. You caught my fish!

Silas pulls his body to one side to steady the boat. Jesus, he says. Only you could accidentally catch a bass. We're losing the light. He pulls a small pipe from his breast pocket. Will you take a hoot?

Sarah lets the bass land against her feet, wet and thrashing. Gestures at the kids.

Right, Silas says. Don't tell Glenna.

I'm more used to close quarters than you are.

So I've heard. You can't even manage a wank. Silas brings the pipe up close with one hand, sparks a lighter with the other. He breathes out and Sarah catches the scent, sweet and charry, but shakes her head.

I manage, she says. But I don't smoke anymore. She picks up the squirming fish and places it in Ruby's lap. He looks just like he's breathing, doesn't he, she says, showing Ruby where the gills are throbbing open. When really he can't breathe at all. Really he's choking.

Silas reaches the pipe toward her and Sarah leaves her hands where they are, on the fish.

The problem is it gives me this intense sense of well-being, she says.

Well, we can't have that.

Really, Sarah says. I can't. It makes it so I can't write.

Because you're not miserable? Silas takes another haul on the pipe, tosses the lighter back in his pocket.

Because I stop asking questions.

What do we do with him now? Ruby says.

We give him a name, Sarah says. And then we throw him back in.

They pull the boat hard up onto shore, Ruby and the boys with wet legs, wading in.

My mommy caught a fish *and* a new fishing rod! Ruby yells to Glenna's mother. She's been waiting to corral the children. There's a fire going at the other end of the beach, Glenna holding Ilsa's baby and Ilsa beckoning to the waders with marshmallows. Sarah lets go of Ruby's hand, walks up to the house. In the kitchen she pours a scotch and fills the sink.

What are you doing? Silas in the doorway.

No-one's touched these, Sarah says, lifting a stack of dirty plates into the water. She doesn't want to say, There's only so much happy family I can take. Squeezes out a measure of dish soap and starts in, cutlery first. Silas picks up her glass and holds it to the light, squinting.

Beckett. I'm so bored. He puts the glass down and leans against the counter.

Then go out to the fire, Sarah says.

You know what I mean.

Sarah rubs at her nose with the sudsy back of her hand, then shakes the soap off into the water. I want to be your friend, she says.

So be my friend. Silas standing there with a green-checked tea towel in his hand. Be my friend, Beckett.

You have everything, Sarah says.

When he leaves she can hear Glenna outside the screen door, pulling him down toward the fire.

Hey, Silas says.

Where the hell are you, Glenna says.

Later Sarah finishes her scotch by the bonfire, and another besides. The men get into the bourbon. She's the last woman standing, all the others in bed or tending babies. Just one shot, Silas begs and she lets him follow her up to the house. He's drunk and holds onto her fingers as they walk inside. He wants to be led by the hand, his fingers curved around hers.

Ruby's hand when I'm walking her to bed, Sarah thinks. When it's dark.

The back of his hand is coarse with short, jutting hairs. Sarah is seized by an urge to squeeze it reassuringly, squeeze until the bones bend and break.

He pours the last of the bourbon into camp mugs.

My wife doesn't like me when you're around, he says.

Sarah picks up her tin mug and twirls, landing unsteadily, one hand on the kitchen counter to stop herself.

Your wife thinks I'm teenager of the year.

Shh, Silas says. You'll wake up the whole house.

Sarah takes herself for a little walk along the counter. I had a house, she says. Remember my house?

It was a great house! Silas lifts his mug in homage to her house.

I know! It was great! We were so great. Everyone thought we were so great. She stops and points a finger at Silas. You think I don't want all this? The finger gyrates, indicating the room, the house. Silas isn't sure. I already did it, Sarah says. She steps forward and lands the finger in the middle of his chest.

I figured we'd be old on a porch, all that garbage, she says. You know how many times I asked him?

To marry you. Silas grabs her mug and takes a sip.

To stop fucking it up.

They drink and Sarah pulls him into the pantry. He's soft, with downy shoulders under his shirt. She doesn't kiss him, but falls to the floor and takes his cock into her mouth and lets the tip slide back against her throat. He tastes the way she expects him to taste: like sweat and sleep and especially urine. When she pulls back he drops down to meet her. She lets him go-to, as if this were his idea, pushing her onto her back, pressing down into her shoulders, one hand pulling at her shorts.

From the floor what she can see is the winter-store: jam and flour, oats, pickles, coffee, rice. Supplies for a reliable place, somewhere to raise children and feed them, fix things that are broken, keep on. The jars and sacks of meal are steady as pictures on the walls, not a permanent record but markers for some future.

Silas presses his mouth on hers. She lets him. It's more or less the same as any other, hard and burnt by alcohol, but when she moves him between her legs he pulls up, giggling, and she can see that he's afraid of her. A sudden memory of another man, also married: when she was eighteen, the sputter of candles in her university residence bedroom. For three months he held her head, wrapped her hand around his cock, but left her clothes on. Told her, I can't be unfaithful. You know how I feel.

She pushes Silas away. The two of them sitting there on the pantry floor and her foot against the bottom of the shelf. A jar falls and lands with a thud. It cracks, rather than sending shards across the room. The sticky insides somehow catch the glass before it has time to smash. Smithereens, Sarah thinks.

She's on her feet, Silas still down on the ground. Beckett, he says. You have pine needles on your bum. This is meant to sound boyish. Threat over. Sarah shoves her shirt into her waistband.

You'd better clean that up, she says, and points to the jam jar. And put your dick away. Your wife is waiting for you.

She walks up to the bunkhouse and he doesn't follow. The beam of the flashlight through the screen. Ruby pulls herself awake. Sarah turns the light off, swishes each foot in the water bucket and opens the door.

There are twenty bears per square kilometre here, Ruby says and closes her eyes again.

Sarah undresses quickly and sits down on the edge of the bed. Their clothes, hers and Ruby's, in a tangle on the floor.

There's a pillow shoved up along the wall that could almost be a body. Sliding into bed with him, faceless him, his blond beard: Sarah thinks of this. The way you can sleep with someone who's been your friend for a long time. The kind of talk, or the quiet fucking reserved for hotel rooms, baby asleep next to you in the collapsible crib.

Well, Sarah thinks. *Do you wait? Do we whisper to each other: Hi Honey how was your day. Your hand up inside my shirt, the newspaper falling aside, do we let it turn dirty. Do you wait?*

She pulls back the sheets. Her notebook. Switches on the little book-light. Ruby's breath comes soft and even. There's the nearly full moon, out on the lake, the screaming loons. In the water bucket by the front door, a white moth.

Sleep World
Zoey Leigh Peterson

Forty-seven minutes is a long time to wait in a mattress store when you don't need a mattress. For the first couple of laps, the salespeople kindly ignore Kathryn. She has explained that she is waiting for someone. It's early on a Tuesday morning, and the salespeople are still handing each other cups of coffee and debriefing on last night's television.

Kathryn wanders the store, trying to look purposeful. She studies each mattress in turn. She contemplates their regal names. She peers into a small cutaway section of mattress with its isolated springs pressed up against the Plexiglas. They look battered and desperate, like the animals in the brochures that still come to the house.

Eventually, one of the young salesmen is sent over to check on her. Kathryn affirms, again, that she is waiting for a friend, that it is the friend who needs a mattress, and that she herself is entirely content with her current mattress, though this is not strictly true. Her own bed is sagging and problematic, but Chris likes it.

The young salesman returns to the pack with this information. They keep talking amongst themselves about this show and that show, but Kathryn can feel them watching her with suspicion. She tries to imagine what they might suspect. That she is going to sneak out of the store with a queen-size box-spring in her bag? That she is going to slit the long, soft belly of a mattress and hide evidence inside? That she is going to move into their showroom with several temperamental cats and set up camp? What is their worst-case scenario?

Now that Sharon owns a car, she is late to everything. The car was part of a story that began with Sharon not having a baby and ended with her and Kyle moving to a condo with cream carpets.

On paper, their new place is not even that far away. A 40-minute ride from Chris and Kathryn's—30 if you really pedal. Kathryn and Sharon had routinely cycled twice that distance when they were in grad school together, but the miles feel somehow longer in this new direction. Bike paths end unceremoniously in the middle of the block, spitting you out onto noisy highways. The cars move faster and seem angrier, and you arrive unhappier than you were when you left.

Back when Sharon and Kyle lived across the alley, the four of them would see each other almost every day. Sometimes to borrow a lemon or envelope or screwdriver, other times because the news was too terrible to watch alone.

Now though, they don't show up at each other's back door with a bottle of wine or half a birthday cake. They don't phone each other and say, We made too much pasta, do you guys want to come eat with us? Instead they say, What does week after next look like? They say, Can we do it at *our* place? They say, Hey I'm coming into town to look at mattresses, why don't you come along and we can catch up.

When Sharon arrives, much is forgiven. The salespeople are not suspicious of Sharon. They are charmed and intrigued by her princess-vs-pea dilemma—a series of fine beds that all felt perfect for the first hour, but then this nagging ache that would creep up her leg and into her spine. It's fun to watch Sharon do her thing. She is getting everyone on board, like they are her students. Kathryn feels lucky to be here with Sharon on a Tuesday morning while her work sits at home on the desk.

Here is what I propose, says Sharon to the gathered sales force. You guys pretend I'm not here and let me lie around in your beds all day like a weirdo. Then at the end of the day, I hand you my credit card and show you the bed you just sold me.

This amuses the salespeople and they bring out special paper booties and special pillows for different kinds of sleepers—side sleepers, stomach sleepers—and a secret notebook with all the pricing information and talking points. And so equipped, Sharon and Kathryn are set adrift in the sea of mattresses.

Okay, says Sharon once they are alone, let's get in bed and then I want to hear all about this Emily thing.

Kathryn had told Sharon about the Emily thing in an inadvertent phone call inspired by Neanderthals. She'd been on the couch watching a BBC program on Neanderthals, the last of a people, and she had suddenly felt so much love for Sharon, and so much longing, that she picked up the phone and dialled the number without thinking.

Sharon was half-watching the same show and paying some bills, and they talked about work for a while and how it must feel for an actor to be cast as a Neanderthal.

Then Sharon had asked what was up, and asked in such a way that Kathryn felt that something should be up. And so, to have something to say, Kathryn told her that Chris had a crush on some Emily from work—which is fine, people get crushes—but that he had invited this person to stay in their apartment while they were away for the long weekend, to house-sit, to sleep in their bed, and that that felt weird. This got Sharon's interest. They talked about it hotly for several minutes—Sharon being emphatic and scandalized in gratifying ways—until Sharon was so sorry, but she had to go to a strata meeting.

Now Sharon is going to want the whole story. Everything is a story now with Sharon. But Kathryn isn't sure what else to say. Chris hasn't mentioned Emily since that weekend. After bringing her up constantly in the weeks leading up to her stay, now he can't even be drawn into conversation about her. When Kathryn asks what Emily looks like or what colour her hair is, Chris can't say. All that Kathryn knows about Emily is what she left behind in their apartment: in the bathroom, a tin of lip balm with a sliding lid that is satisfying to open and close; in the recycling, a half-rinsed jar of some paste that makes the whole house smell velvety; in the bedroom, nothing, although both their clock radios were unplugged; and on the refrigerator, a three page letter of thanks, politely addressed to both of them, but clearly written for Chris and filled with such candour and fellowship that it felt too intimate to read. Kathryn had read it twice. All this she has already told Sharon on the phone while the Neanderthals failed to adapt.

Kathryn considers now telling Sharon about the misspellings in the letter, not just Kathryn's name, but in almost every line. But she cannot think of a way to say this without feeling dirty. Finally, she resolves to say this: There is no story. There are just these feelings that come and go. Feelings without a beginning, middle, and end.

But by the time they are settled into a bed, they are already talking about sex.

Since buying the condo, Sharon and Kyle have been out of sync, sexually. Morning has always been their time. Truthfully, morning and night. But especially morning. These days, though, Kyle's brain wakes up making lists and doesn't remember it has a body until it's time to leave for work. Now Sharon has found a solution: Oats before bed. Apparently, half a cup of Scottish uncut oats right before bed has Kyle waking up like his former self.

That's why I was late getting here, Sharon says. She doesn't actually wink.

Kathryn rolls onto her side and stares out over the empty mattresses. They're like ice floes. Can you steer an ice floe? Or do you just go where it takes you?

How did you figure that out, Kathryn asks. The oat thing.

Ann-Marie, from our building, she told me about it, says Sharon.

Kathryn has met this Ann-Marie, once, at Sharon and Kyle's housewarming. Ann-Marie was in the kitchen blending margaritas and warming tortillas in a cast-iron pan she'd brought from her place across the hall. Let me take that, said Ann-Marie, plucking a dirty plate from Kathryn's hand. This kitchen is exactly like mine, so I already know my way around, said Ann-Marie, though Kathryn could see the sink right there.

You should try it, says Sharon of the oats. This, Kathryn understands, is a reference to Chris, and Kathryn feels a vague urge to defend him.

Chris has what Kathryn calls a high cuddle drive. He kisses her awake every morning, he reaches out to touch her arm while they read the paper, he hugs her for whole minutes, which she loves. But sex, when it comes, comes in slippers. Still, over the years they have found a sort of equilibrium. And it's nice, the sex, when they have it.

This isn't working for me, says Sharon, rising from the bed. Too mooshy, she says.

They drift through the beds, Sharon pressing her palm firmly down into each mattress and holding it there, eyes closed, as if communing with the bed's essential nature. Kathryn looks at price tags. Some of the beds are so unaccountably expensive, that Kathryn—if it was up to her—wouldn't even pause in front of them, wouldn't give them the satisfaction.

Sharon is lingering over a four-thousand-dollar bed. She has slid her hand under the foam pad and is palpating the springs, dispassionately, like a doctor. She is in fact a middle-school teacher.

Didn't they just buy a bed, Sharon and Kyle? (Kathryn remembers precisely: It was an engagement present to themselves.) Did they sell that bed? Where does four thousand dollars come from? How do you buy a condo, and then a bed, and then another bed?

There was a time when she might have asked Sharon these questions. Actually, there was a time she wouldn't have *had* to ask—the answers would have bubbled to the surface while they helped each other put away groceries or stood in line together to cash their student loans. When they were part of the slow unspooling of each other's lives.

Sharon has sunk herself into the four-thousand-dollar mattress. Kathryn is converting the price in her head. Four thousand dollars is her food for an entire year. It is the dental work Chris needs. It is x hours of copy-editing plus y hours of indexing, over the ten-year life of the bed, for a total of z hours per year. Kathryn climbs into the exquisite bed.

Sharon holds Kathryn's hand as they lie staring up at the acoustic panels.

This is the one, Sharon says. Her hand feels softer than it used to, and bigger, in a four-thousand-dollar bed.

Sharon used to be cheap. When they were students, when money was a thing, Sharon was flamboyantly frugal, a loud champion of all things scrounged or redeemed.

One time, Sharon and Kyle had shown up at their door late one evening, exultant, because the video store was throwing out old VHS tapes. Sharon had rescued *The Great Muppet Caper* from a cardboard box on the sidewalk, just as the rain was starting to fall.

Chris pulled the futon off the frame and onto the living-room floor, and the four of them sardined themselves under two overlapping blankets and watched and cheered and made amazing jokes, until Kathryn thought she might hyperventilate.

Later, exhausted by their own hilarity, they watched in silence, a blissful stupor washing over their bodies. And Kathryn loved these people, loved living on this futon island with them, and it was at this moment—as the movie rounded into the third act—that Kathryn began to think about the four of them falling asleep here in front of the TV, and the four of them waking up in the morning and making breakfast together and deciding what to do with their Sunday, the four of them. Kyle was already drifting off, soughing faintly between songs. And then Chris was asleep, furrowing and scrunching his sincere face. And then it was just Sharon and Kathryn holding hands and fading in and out as the tireless puppets saved the day. Then the credits were rolling and Sharon was squeezing her hand, then letting it go. She was reaching for Kyle's shoulder, rubbing him slowly awake.

You guys can stay, Kathryn had said. You should stay.

Sharon smiled, and kept rousing Kyle, who made a low, assenting rumble.

You should stay, Kathryn said again. It felt urgent.

But now Kyle was standing up, his eyes still closed, and Sharon was leading him to the door.

Thank you for a perfect night, Sharon said.

Kathryn locked the door behind them and stood there trying to reabsorb her feelings. She could hear Chris stirring in the other room. He was calling out to her—making an endearing joke that had threaded through the evening—and she was suddenly irritated and hot and a kind of angry that she could not name. She did not answer. She washed the dishes loudly and wrestled the futon back onto the frame and did not go to bed until Chris was surely asleep. And by the next day, Sharon and Kyle were engaged.

This, ladies, is as good as it gets. So says the salesman. The reigning king of beds, he says. He begins to enumerate the many features of this noble mattress. Kathryn can see the contents of his nostrils.

They have only been in this bed for half an hour, and Kathryn waits for Sharon to drive the salesman away, remind him of their deal. But Sharon does not drive him away. She encourages him. She calls him Gary, which is his name. She asks Gary how long the warranty is, she asks about coil count. They talk admiringly to each other about the bed while Kathryn stares into a halogen light. She is thinking again about that letter, magneted to her fridge.

And what do you think, the salesman asks Kathryn. Kathryn doesn't understand the question.

She's just keeping me company, Sharon says, letting go of Kathryn's hand. Sharon explains to the salesman that her boyfriend—fiancé actually—can sleep on anything and so bed-shopping with him is impossible because he dozes off on every bed they try.

The salesman makes a half-neutered observation about men and women and Sharon laughs. Sharon and the salesman begin to rehearse the differences between men and women.

But Chris would be here. If Kathryn had a pain in her leg, if Kathryn was unable to sleep at night, Chris would be here beside her, even if he was bored. But he wouldn't be bored. He would be engaged. He would make it into a game. He would make up life-stories for each mattress. He would tell her about their childhoods as beanbags, imbuing each bed with hopes and ambitions and tragic flaws that he and Kathryn might recognize and grow to love. And Kathryn would mostly listen, but would occasionally blurt out some bit of business that he would seamlessly integrate into the story.

And when the time came to decide, Chris would listen to her messy, rambling anxieties about where the bed was made, what the factory conditions were for the workers, and did she really need a new bed at all, and didn't most of the world sleep on mats not half as comfortable as the bed they already had. And when she got overwhelmed by the morality of it and all the choices and the expense and the materialism and she started to panic, he would put his arm around her and guide her out of the store and across the street to the Chinese place and he would order dumplings and put them in front of her. And he would sit there and take all the terror and despair and just surround it with his goodness and absorb it like charcoal until she could stand herself again and could go back across the street and buy a bed. And when some salesman told them that men are like this and women are like that, she would know that she and Chris were on the same side and that Gary was on the other. Because she and Chris are a team.

Sharon is sitting up now, digging through her bag. She is buying the four-thousand-dollar bed. Kathryn wonders at the quiet snap of this decision. How one minute Sharon did not know, and then the next minute she did. It is only 11:30 in the morning.

Kathryn has not said any of the things she meant to say. She meant to say that, yes, the thought of Emily eats at her. That she feels colonized by that letter, planted like a flag in her kitchen. That sometimes when she comes home and the letter has been moved slightly, she wishes that Emily would disappear and have never existed, but that sometimes she wishes it was Chris who would disappear, or she herself, or that nobody had ever existed and the planet was still choked with algae and God was pleased. Other times, she hears some dumb song on the radio that makes her feel connected to everything—mattress salesmen and deer ticks and crying babies—and she wants Chris to do whatever he needs to be happy. If he needs to kiss Emily, then kiss her. Or worse. She just wants him to be happy. She wants him to be happy so he can make *her* happy.

Sometime this week would be ideal, says Sharon.

Sharon has her day-planner out, making arrangements for the mattress to be delivered. Kathryn gazes blankly at the appointments and the half-familiar names. It's mostly wedding stuff. Then she sees her own name:

Sleep World
(w/Kathryn!)

Next to her name is drawn a small heart. The whole day is blocked off. Kathryn wonders if they will now have lunch and sit on some heated patio drinking bellinis and talking about big and small things, or if the unexpected efficiency of her purchase will inspire Sharon to see how many other tasks she can accomplish today.

Kathryn doesn't mind either way. She is ready to go home. She has something to say to Chris. It is starting to take up space in her mouth. She wants him to be happy. What is her worst-case scenario?

Addresses
Cynthia Flood

The *right* apartment. Meaning what?

For Julie, that Jeremy be in it.

He did the hunting. Often she came along, still happy though sickish-dazed from The Pill.

Distinctive 1 BR suite even had a pantry. They moved in.

By then Julie could, just, see around him.

Also she knew she had never filled Jeremy's vision.

Sort-of arguments began, about The Pill. After research that took a lot of time away from his work, he decided on condoms and foam.

In the distinctive building's entry, ceramic tiles were octagons in a complex black-and-white arrangement. There was stained glass and no elevator. No laundry-room. The brass door-plates and fir floors were original.

"I checked." Satisfied, Jeremy closed the pantry door to work for hours so they could get ahead.

The paned windows stood tall, Julie not. They and the floors gleamed (she made sure of that), yet the elegant life once lived in these turn-of-the-century Vancouver rooms did not seem like anything she could match.

"What about a baby?"

"No, not yet. "

"When?"

"Not yet!"

Every time, Julie did not start a third interchange. Did she lack character? She hungered for concord. They settled, kind of, on *Soon*.

To be alone so much was still surprising. The magazines sug-

gested picking one room each day, in rotation, for special cleaning. Julie did that. She ordered dress-patterns, clipped recipes.
Dinner was quite good sometimes. When Jeremy stayed late at
the law office she'd get into bed to wait, wanting him.

The spermicidal foam oozed all over the bed-linen. Back and
forth Julie walked to the laundromat, never meeting the same
people there.

"You're pregnant?"

Jeremy couldn't or wouldn't believe she hadn't tricked him.

"Got your way, again." He slapped at the want ads, some red-
circled. "I have no time for this. Can you at least follow up?"

Did *again* mean he hadn't wanted to marry?

Julie followed up, went further.

Of the place she found, he said, "It'll do for the time being."

What could time do but be?

Jeremy conceded the value of *2 BR, nr shops, bus, beach*, although old frame houses with lacy trim had been bulldozed to
make space for the *mod apt tower*. He deplored and Julie smiled
at the lobby's earnest mural of a tropical sunset, the palm trees
etched on the mirror by the mailboxes.

Of *1 prkg* he said, "Too bad you were careless. No money for
that now."

Their own decor did please him. All paint and textiles and
floor-coverings were bone. Not the red lumps that dogs gnaw
on, Julie knew that. White trim.

"Perfect neutrals. You do see how they don't call attention to
themselves?"

The look of their Danish coffee table by the picture window
also pleased Jeremy, for the north-east light enhanced the teak's
grain. He removed their white cups to the kitchen as soon as
they were empty.

"If only we were higher up." He opened his briefcase.

Under new mgmt.

"That's you!" Silently Julie teased the hidden kicking child.
"You get the second BR." Jeremy's desk, electric typewriter, file
cabinet lived in the master.

The elevator too was soundless. Eyes closed, Julie couldn't
tell whether the movement was up or down. The little tale she
made of this uncertainty failed to amuse her husband after his

stressful day in court.

"Do you mean that?" Jeremy asked.

He asked the question again when the baby's crying made Julie worry about the neighbours. "This building's solid concrete. I guess construction is another thing you just can't understand?"

Still Julie couldn't forget his pallor after the delivery, his joyful tears as he phoned long-distance to tell his parents and hers about James, while she trembled after a labour not much like that in the natural childbirth book.

Nor did she forget how they two began, at her *sunny Kits bach gt view*. Unusually for a girl, she'd had her own apartment. Jeremy had been surprised.

As Julie walked home from her little job in the weeks before their wedding, the pavement went all wavery rivery till she sped like a hydrofoil to the soaring elevator, the hall, her own door, and the engulfing heat of Jeremy's body. She'd been the initiator. He, taken aback. Shocked? Julie, though her mother and all the books warned against pre-marital activity, knew no doubt.

What was that view, anyway? The only one of her class to leave Victoria after secretarial school, she was just proud to have her own address.

Perhaps the sex was why the ceremony didn't change her?

After their honeymoon at Expo 67, the Kitsilano place felt cramped, wrong. Not even a nook for Jeremy's work.

He found, first, the *stately spacious 1 BR*. This was at a good address, a fine old Dunbar mansion chopped into suites. Tall beautiful trees made the place dark. Leaking radiators, mice. Julie and Jeremy shivered till he located the *distinctive* building.

"Where we'd still be, if you hadn't been careless."

She didn't remember much about Expo either. The hotel room. Fireworks, sugar, glitter, crowds. French actually spoken.

Now this high-rise.

The developer had built three towers close together, so Jeremy and Julie's living-room in The Buckingham observed one in The Kensington where sofa, stereo, TV, and coffee table were similarly configured. The occupants were two men. Older, Julie thought, early forties.

The man with curly hair sometimes waved at the baby. Julie

would raise James's tiny hand, smile. The overweight man didn't wave. If he noticed her across the airy gap he snapped the Venetians shut, even in sunshine.

Jeremy did the same. "I'm not paying rent to watch a couple of queers day in day out. We need our own house."

More things Julie hadn't understood.

James filled her hours. His certainty amazed her. *Now!* He cried with his mouth so wide his throat was a quivering red tunnel.

The neighbours Julie encountered in the elevator and by the mailbox were mostly retirees with little dogs, or young singles. Once just heading out of the lobby was a bald man in crisp shirt and shorts who held a placard, *Out Of Vietnam Now!* Wasn't that an American war? He strode away. Was he old? Seeking other mums, she pushed James's stroller along the concrete walkway by Sunset Beach.

At the inadequate corner grocery she met the queers. Sam held back at first while Curly warned her never to buy the ground beef, but soon all three were picking through the faded vegetables together. Walking back, they smiled at the towers' palatial names.

One morning in The Buckingham's laundry-room, Julie was giving James his bottle while waiting for the dryer to finish.

An old woman came in and smiled at the baby. "It is my lucky day! Mostly the people here have these foolish dogs. But you do not breast-feed? Is best."

Julie explained the theory of parents sharing equally in baby-care. Under-thoughts about Jeremy rushed counter to her words.

In her tailored maroon dress, Mrs Schatz moved about briskly, high heels clicking. Her wrinkles broke into new webs when she looked at James.

"So, how you like it here?" she asked. "What floor?"

The Schatzes lived on the view side of the eleventh.

"We will drink coffee. My husband will like to see James. Also I will invite Mr Alexander, on the sixth. He appreciates art."

Before that happened, Julie met Sam and Curly again.

This was at Sunset Beach, in the pause when the bridge's lamps begin to reflect on the greying water yet daylight still hovers over False Creek, stippling the waves pink or apricot.

Under a fine rain they ambled talking along the pebbled sands. James, held in his Snugli against Julie's warmth, kept tilting his head back to get the drops on his face. He smiled. So did Curly and Sam and Julie.

"How did you meet?" she asked when they left the beach. The bridge lamps were now shedding gold circles on the salty darkness.

The men exchanged looks and snickered, snapping the Venetians down. Both spoke. At last Curly managed, "We'd both been around enough to know what we wanted. We were ready."

As Julie with James rode up in the air she thought how the magazines said things just like that, about deciding in the right way to get married.

"Where've you been? You're soaked. No umbrella again?"

She described their pleasant walk.

Jeremy made a face. "Queers are useless. That's why I don't like them."

"Is a tax accountant useless?"

"Who does Fatty work for? Other queers? And what does Pretty Boy do?'

Julie quit, though in fact Curly was the numbers guy and Sam the waiter.

"We need to get out. This isn't what I had in mind." He shoved a newspaper at her and stood waiting by the door into the master.

After skimming *Houses* Julie studied *Furnished Suites.* Some buildings said *Small child accepted.* What size might that be? How could she pay? She perused *Board & Room.* Water dripped off her hair on to the baby's smile.

"Nothing today."

The door closed. Shut out.

Now Julie did feel changed, though she still waited greedily for Jeremy to come to bed. Sometimes he slept on the sofa.

Time went on being.

James grew bigger, bigger. With pain he acquired teeth. He looked about, inquiring. He shook and pulled at his playpen's bars. Visiting the eleventh floor, he demonstrated how he would crawl soon.

Mr Schatz chuckled. "He reminds me."

"Mr Alexander is tired today. He fights cancer," his wife sighed. She pointed at the tiny poppyseed pastries veiled in powdered sugar. "His favourites." For James she had baked rusks.

"He also is exile by a war," said her husband.

From the Schatzes' windows, the distant Olympic Mountains shimmered aquamarine. The stereo was playing classical. Nearer, Mount Baker shone like pearl. Victoria was clouded in drifts of white, invisible.

On leaving, Julie was revolted at the prospect of entering the apartment where she lived. She pressed James's thumb on L for Lobby.

By the mailboxes stood the bald man. He held a map.

"An impossible city," he said. "Vancouver's a simple place, the mountains are always north. Even New York's mostly a grid."

He was Julie's age. So thin in his sharply pressed Bermudas, paler even than bone. The map showed London, England.

"Are you going there?"

"Paris too. New York on the way back, if I'm not arrested." He tucked the map into a travel agent's folder. "See the galleries one more time."

"Are you Mr Alexander?"

"Gary."

"Julie. This is James."

"Dear Mrs Schatz," he said, "always wanting to feed me. Their sadness is unbearable, but I'll see them before I go."

"I hope you have a good time." What else could be said?

"Thank you." He inspected the baby. "Such sharp teeth! A little animal. So Julie, where are you off to?"

After a moment she said, "I have no idea."

Gary's eyebrows went up. "Better get one! Up and down, to and fro, then suddenly it's all over."

They shook hands warmly.

Soon after this, Jeremy began again about the oral contraceptive.

"You have to. We can't risk it. I insist."

Three things just like that with no breath between.

"You know it makes me sick." In disbelief she heard the shaking voice.

"Then I won't have sex with you."

After that there was only the morning dialogue before he departed for office or court.

"Will you?"

"No." Again, again. "*No.*" Julie gripped James so he howled and shoved his head into her armpit.

In the mirror, her lipstick looked wrong for the face she had now.

She still longed for sex with that changed man.

Or had the persons called *Julie & Jeremy* not ever recognized each other?

Had two others used their names to get married? She winced.

Daily his mother pushed James for hours through the West End to see the lines of bright windows in high-rises, low-rises, and to imagine their views. The Buckingham, later, seemed like nowhere she'd visited before.

Gary was in London now. He stood alert in front of paintings. On the postcard he sent, a stern man wore olive and brown. Why was he painted? She did not show the card to Jeremy.

Mrs Schatz said, "That is Bacon."

James stayed with her once while Julie went out to walk alone, a novelty. Along Denman and Davie streets she examined closely what was on offer in each store window. On her return the child's lips were red with happy jam.

"Must he go?" asked Mr Schatz. Julie didn't tell that either.

Every day she and Jeremy did the dialogue.

Every day she feared saying, "All right, I'll do it."

And his loud voice shook. "I'm never having sex with you." Was the assertion wearing thin? Fear grew. She tried to imagine telling this. Who could hear? Mum, unthinkable. Her high school friends in Victoria knew nothing, were only engaged. In that too she'd led the way.

One morning Julie was so terrified that she pulled a dress over her head and gathered up James and went barefoot down to the beach.

The tide was ebbing; the water went west in a silver rush. In her arms the baby strove to move freely. Every pebble had a different shape. They hurt her feet. Why had she got married? When would Gary die? A dog chased sticks, plunged into and out of the water, shook rainbows. Julie waded. Cold first, then refreshing. She held James so his toes dangled in the waves. He kicked, chuckled. A long time went by, a short time.

Back at the palace, Julie pressed B and prayed.

She was folding her husband's socks.

"How is Mr Beautiful?" Mrs Schatz inspected Julie. "Rose is a good colour for you. Also it is a shade never out of style. But you do not wear shoes today?"

"In a hurry." Julie couldn't articulate.

"To leave. I see." Mrs Schatz's manicured fingers stroked James's tender hair. "Sometimes is best."

Julie carried the wicker laundry-basket out to the elevator.

"Thank you, my dear. You know where to find me." Today her smart outfit was in navy. Every curl lay in place. How could she and Gary look so neat?

Julie whispered, "I do."

"Be careful," said Mrs Schatz, and disappeared.

Jeremy had gone to his work.

James banged and grumbled in his pen while Julie did hers. With Dutch Cleanser on a toothbrush she toured the base of the toilet. At the sink, her Q-Tip winkled out guerrilla dirt-specks crouching where faucet met porcelain. She emptied the medicine cabinet, washed each glass shelf. One hand took up a remnant disk of The Pill. Five pink, twenty blue, each snug in its cell. Then a glass of water was in her other hand.

"Can't risk it," she said to James, who screamed at her from behind his bars. "We must be careful."

Soon Julie visited her doctor. Graciously he renewed her prescription but gave her a critical look.

Jeremy asked later, "Can't you even button your blouse right?"

The card Mr Alexander sent the Schatzes from Paris showed a sculpture of a pregnant goat. She looked lustful and witty.

Mrs Schatz said, "He says he will go home very soon. His lady-friend from before has a place in Ithaca, New York. He can be ill there."

War, love, art, cancer. How did someone her age get such a history?

Though swallowing eagerly, Julie still defied her husband.

149

His daily shouts seemed an omen of rape. Were they both crazy? She had no answers, only a baby.

In James's room stood a chaise-longue for night feedings. Julie now slept there. Once crying wakened her, but James was asleep. Another time, getting up to pee, she saw Jeremy prone on the sofa. Their own double bed was smooth, its pillows plump. None of this could be in any magazine.

Julie took James to visit her old workplace.

Wanting to look well, she wore her rose dress. Its length was out of style, she saw on reaching the office. Julie told various lies while she and the girls had their happy time catching up in the coffee-room, the table a cosy dither of cookies and doughnuts and James's applesauce.

Julie's replacement was friendly. They giggled together over the manager's limited Dictaphone skills.

He himself was amiable, tickling her boy under the chin. "You got a really important job here, Julie!"

Then the girls must get back to work.

The bus-stop was across the road that once led to *sunny Kits bach*. Headache. Exhaustion. No umbrella. The bus was slow to arrive, slow crossing the bridge. James squalled and flailed as they neared The Buckingham, not the right place, Julie knew that at least, though in the downpour she couldn't find her keys, scrabbled in her purse again, couldn't, was spiralling into a tizzy when Sam and Curly appeared.

"Come up to our place."

The Kensington's murals showed Mediterranean waters of a sultry indigo not possible to imagine in English Bay.

"What's in The Windsor's lobby, I wonder?"

"We got in, to look. South-west," Curly answered. "Reds, pinks."

"Your elevator's quiet too," Julie remarked.

"Yes. Hard to tell if it's up or down."

As they started along the hall, Sam gestured toward their door but stopped himself. "Of course you know your way, Julie!"

When he took off his hooded rain-jacket, on one temple was revealed a large bruise. Julie didn't ask. He pointed. "You'd think they'd attack Curly, he's so cute, but more often it's me. Because I've got him, I guess."

After his bottle, James slept among the sofa cushions. Julie found her keys. Curly brought coffee, shoving comics and beer cans away to make room for the tray. Sam smoked. Julie took her first cigarette since meeting Jeremy.

In their bathroom were far more bottles tubes jars than she and he owned. His contempt twanged in her ear. On the door hung two silky robes. Emerging, she managed a glance into the bedroom. The mattress was bare, with fresh folded linen stacked ready.

"We'd like to paint it purple," Sam said, "but when we go we'd just have to do that boring beige again."

"Go where?"

"We're planning to buy a house."

Curly chuckled. "To be as purple as we like." He touched Sam's head.

Back in the living-room, Julie collected her essentials. How strange, to look out from here toward her present address. Not that there was much to see. In the suite below, a coffee-table displayed a big platter, elliptical and brightly glazed. It drew her eye.

Mrs Schatz stood in The Buckingham's lobby, dressed for lunching out. That morning the expected news had arrived from Ithaca. Also the Schatzes had decided to get a little dog, to care for.

We Are All Illegals
Clark Blaise

Pramila came down from Palo Alto to deliver what she calls a "probabalistic algorithm" for me to beat Stanford's #1 seed, Mike Mahulkar. She's been scouting Mike's game, mathematically. She's sure of her algorithm, but I'm the variable. I don't know why she wants to help me, but nothing about her surprises me.

She's in Stanford's on-line "Gifted" program, and she'll be going full-time to the real Stanford next fall, when she's thirteen years, ten months old. With all her AP credits, she'll enter as a junior. I'm five years older, but next year I'll just be a sophomore at Santa Cruz. She'll have her Master's by the time I graduate. Of course, thirteen of her years are like 50 of anyone else's.

I hadn't seen her since Christmas break. Two months ago, Dad was still at home but plotting to go back to India. Ma was still working at Stanford Library. Pram was still ice-skating. Now she's buzz-cut her hair and she's not skating and she's thinner and smaller than I remember. She said Ma's cut her hair real short, a pixie cut, and she's dyeing it blacker than Pram's. The Big Cat's gone to India so the mice will play. He hated short hair. He dyed his own hair but he disapproved of women who changed their looks. My Palo Alto life and all its routines have receded. College wipes out everything. I barely remember the house I lived in for most of my life.

Pram's algorithm says that after seven consecutive base line drives to Mike's backhand, he'll will start lifting his returns. "Imperceptible to you, probably," she says, but if I trust her, "measurably." Don't let him shift his feet. Keep him in a backhand stance. After his ninth, there'll also a drop in pace, setting himself up for my best forehand slam. "Just don't be your usual greedy self and go to your forehand too early."

My father always admired Mike Mahulkar—or to use his so-called "good name"—Mukesh. Why couldn't I be more like Mukesh Mahulkar? My girlfriend Anya is Russian and used to date Mike until Dr. Mahulkar went back to Bombay and interviewed 50 of the richest and prettiest girls in the city and finally found The Blessed One to bring back—Europe-educated, prominent family, a multilingual skier and golfer, socially sophisticated and caste-appropriate for marriage. Anya was reduced to practice-partner. I know Mike Mahulkar well enough to hate him. When he was a sophomore at Stanford and I was a senior at Palo High, he threw me a few dollars a week as a lob-and-volley partner. He could beat me easily then, but he's not as good as he thinks.

So Mike, "The Mumbai Miracle," "The Bombay Bomber," went on to the NCAA championship last year and with a little luck I won the Cal State high school title and got a scholarship to UC-Santa Cruz. Nothing would please me more than beating Mike Mahulkar, but my father probably wouldn't even hear about it. I'd love to be able to mention, casually, at some time in the future if I ever go to India, Oh, by the way, I beat your precious Mukesh Mahulkar. Rubbed his face in that acrylic-covered concrete Stanford mush. Bounced his little head on the fake-grass plastic. Sorry you didn't see it. Sorry you never saw Anya and me together. You made me need to hide her.

"Who's the chick?" asked Arvind, my roommate, when Pramila went to the bathroom. "She's hot, dude."

"She's no chick, RV. She's my sister and she's thirteen."

RV squints at me. "Thirteen's good," he says. "Low-hanging fruit, I'd take a bite. You've seen my sister. Twenty-four and a fat hog."

Dorm-chatter. Arvind's never had a date in his life. He expects his poor father to schlep off to India and find him a wife. If he actually called Pram, I'd wring his neck. I've seen his sister, and she's no hog. Maybe no great blonde Sharapova like my Anya, but she'll make a decent match with someone, probably Indian, although 24 is getting on.

Pram wants to talk, and to see Monterey Bay, so we drive down to Cliff Drive. Santa Cruz is quite the campus: always sunny, with forests, bike trails, the Santa Cruz Boardwalk and the Pacific. It's February, but warm and sunny, T-shirt and flip-flop weather.

"I saw whales last week," I say, which isn't exactly true, but I try hard to transcend the boring trivia of my life. Tennis practice, lifting and running four hours a day, classes that don't spark much interest, evenings with Arvind and his dumb friends, and weekends with Anya when she decides to come down from Stanford. So we park and take a bench and I think it's going to be a friendly little chat but she ignores my whale-talk and raises the ante.

"Ma's having an affair," she says.

Unbelievable. "Who with?"

She rolls her eyes, which means I've just stepped in it. "That is so typical of you. I try to share something important and all you want to know is who's to blame? I really don't care who it is. If you haven't noticed, our family is falling apart and everyone is running for shelter. Ma's found hers and I've got mine and you should be finding yours."

I want to say, I don't believe you. I believe the affair—that's hard to hide. But you don't know who she's doing it with? You've just stumbled onto the first problem in your whole genius life that you haven't been able to solve with a snap of your fingers, so you pretend it doesn't matter. It's not stupid to wonder *who*? And who or what is *your* "shelter"? Math? Ice-skating? Why did you quit the skating? And why did you cut your hair so short, and why don't you eat more? You're melting away. You frighten me.

Our father has been in India for eight weeks, and none of us thinks he's coming back. None of us wants him to. He says he's on the verge of landing A Big Job and when he sends the word, he expects Ma and Pram to go back to India. He'll be in for a big surprise. Pram would have to give up Stanford and enter some sort of convent school where they don't teach the higher math. Ma would give up her lover, whoever he is. I left India when I was nearly four years old and I haven't been back. Even when the others went for funerals or weddings, they kept me back in Palo Alto staying with a sitter.

"Do you ever think all of this——" and she makes a sweeping gesture to include the trails, the Boardwalk, the bluff we're sitting on, the town, the ocean—"could just suddenly vanish?"

Frankly, no, I don't. But to play along I say, "Like a sharp knife cutting through a slice of wedding cake?" She keeps staring out to sea, silently. So I continue, "We're in California. The ocean is rising. They find new fault-lines every few weeks, and The Big One is overdue." Still silent. Maybe she feels microtremors underfoot, like a dog or a cat.

"Something like that," she says.

"I can drive you back to Palo Alto," I say. Maybe she'll open up on the ride and I'll find out a little more. I figure it's someone she works with at Stanford Library.

"Mr. Borisov drove me down, and he's waiting around the Boardwalk to take me back."

Mr. Borisov, better known as Borya, is her skating coach. What I've observed over the past couple of years is that when she refers to him as "Mr. Borisov" and not Borya, she's trying create the impression of distance between them. If he's her shelter, he's three times her age.

Suddenly, she's all smiles—twinkly and innocent—that means insincerity. She asks, "So how's your Golden Goddess?"

"Anya's great. She's coming down tomorrow."

"Borya says she belongs in a fur hat and black sable coat like Julie Christie in *Dr. Zhivago*."

Whatever that means.

She swings her legs, folds and unfolds her hands. As suddenly as it came, the smile drains away. Now she's frowning. Still worrying about the slumping coastline? Maybe she's feeling microtremors.

"Maybe she should wait," she says. Then she starts walking down to the Boardwalk, and motions for me to follow. On the way down she says, "I won't tell Ma about your Russian if you don't tell her about mine."

A few minutes later we're at a little coffee shop, drinking smoothies, waiting for Borya. She says, "You have my Mahulkar algorithm. Now I have to ask a favour from you."

"Anything," I say.

"Be careful with that. I'd like you to come up to Stanford today. They want you to take a test and you can stay the night at home. Borya can drive you back tomorrow."

I'm about to say, I'd like to, but I've got tennis practice. Then something holds me back. It's a flattering notion, that Stanford wants me, but I'm not Stanford material. Without tennis, I might not even have made it into UC-SC. But I'm still smiling, thinking of taking a test at Stanford, maybe even a "Stupid Older Brothers of Genius Sisters" test.

"What kind of test?" Maybe it's a tennis tryout. Maybe they want me.

And then I could read her face, or at least her eyes. If they're windows on the soul, I'm looking into black holes, no light bounces back.

"In the last few weeks, I haven't been feeling good. I've been getting weaker after every practice. Finally I called Dr. Gupta and he referred me to someone at SU Hospital. That was two days ago and I'm going in for my first round of chemo this afternoon."

"Wait," I say. "You have leukaemia?"

"A little bit, yes."

She can say all this lightly, matter-of-factly. "You and me, there're no two people closer on the planet—haematologically speaking." She wriggles her fingers in front of my face. "I'll be your vampire-bride, sucking up your blood with a side-dish of marrow. Sends chills down your spine, just thinking about it, right?" Then, back to business. "It's just a little test. Just in case the chemo doesn't take and I need a transplant. It won't interfere with your tennis."

The real fact is—for all the pain we've caused each other, and for the pain in the ass she can be, and the standards she sets that I can't live up to—I love her. She already is my vampire-bride. We've been more than compatible. I don't care about beating Mike Mahulkar. The thought of losing her is something I can't live with.

Borya enters. He is a small man from Minsk with close-cropped hair and a greying moustache. "You have talked?" he asks her, and she nods. "So now we go to hospital?" and he twirls a set of car-keys.

On the way up the coast highway, I watch how they sit in the front seat. They fit together. I've never had that sense of belonging. And I realize I don't have it with Anya, either. Maybe I'm sensing what Pram felt about Ma, a special new way of sitting, a new way of talking, maybe a new way of dressing. Different foods. Cutting her hair short and dyeing it.

Her name is Dr. Veena Gopalan, and she's on the staff of Paediatric Haematology and Oncology. My parents always had Indian doctors, Indian dentists, Indian lawyers and Indian accountants. If my father could have found Indian mechanics, housepainters and pizza deliverers, he would have had them, too. Not from chauvinism, he would say—just because Indians had higher bars to climb, and were, therefore, like himself, better in their professions than anyone else except maybe the Chinese.

I'm struck by the word. Not "Oncology" which is frightening enough, but "Paediatric." Pram, who's never been a child, never been treated as a child, who's never met a problem she couldn't solve, is suddenly just that: a child, facing a challenge she might not defeat.

They've already taken her away. She's being prepped. I squeezed her hand—the last time I'll be able to touch her, she says, at least for a few days. Borya put his hand on her spiky hair. When she comes out again, after the chemo, they'll put her in a sterile room. Now Borya sits alone in the outer room with his head in his hands. Many parents sit on the sofas with their heads in their hands.

Dr. Gopalan, short, stout and jowly, takes me into her office. She explains the procedures, as she calls them. Pram was definitively diagnosed two days ago. They'd wanted to start treatment on the spot, but she'd asked for a day in order to finish an assignment, then go down to Santa Cruz and bring me back with her. "She's a remarkable young lady, and she wanted you to be near her. She wanted to be the one to tell you. You and that Russian seem to be her chosen family."

"And our mother?" I ask.

"Yes, of course. She will also come around, when she can."

I ask about the compatibility test, but Dr. Gopalan waves it off. "It's only a precaution. We can test for compatibility any time. Siblings have the best chance for compatibility. We hope she goes into remission immediately. If she does not, then we will consider a transplant. We have discussed all the options and the likely outcome. She even calculated her odds of survival."

Another algorithm.

On the drive up to Stanford from Santa Cruz, I kept flashing back to the one thing I remember from India. I was three, and Ma and I went to crazy-loud and crazy-crowded Crawford Market to buy our suitcase. It must have been the first time I'd been let out of my grandmother's flat. I must have been speaking Marathi since I had yet to hear a word of English, and now I can't remember a word of Marathi, except for foods and what I pick up around the house when my parents are arguing.

That day, my father had finally sent for us from California. He'd found an affordable house and he'd finished his doctorate. He had a Green Card and a good job at PacBell and for me he said he'd seen cowboys and Indians, so I felt I needed to arrive in California with a cowboy hat. I'd never seen my father except in photos. He'd gone back to California right after the marriage. My father was a far-off god, just an all-powerful rumour who sent us money.

Finding an authentic cowboy hat in Bombay was a challenge, especially since no-one knew what a cowboy hat looked like, but if one existed anywhere in India it would be in Crawford Market where just about every piece of unsold merchandise in the world ended up under dust and cobwebs. And so the prize was eventually found and dusted off: a red cowboy hat, child-size, with the name Dale Evans written in white ink across the brim.

That's what I was wearing when we landed in San Francisco. That's what I slept in that first night, dreaming of cowboys and Indians, when my father wasn't there to meet us.

He told me once that his greatest shame was missing our arrival. He'd been at the international arrivals of San Francisco airport in plenty of time, but his view all the arrivals half-hidden between stacked boxes and suitcases was blocked, and of course he'd never seen me and a little boy in a red cowboy hat was the last thing he'd be looking for, and Ma wasn't in a sari as he'd been expecting. She'd gone out and bought "American" slacks and a sweater. Very risky behaviour, now that I think about it. I'd even cried when I saw her out of a sari for the first time. He'd heard the public announcement: "Dr. Vivek Waldekar, please pick up the white courtesy telephone for an important message."

But he hadn't picked it up because he wasn't white, and it shocked him that racialist nonsense was part of his new home. From the very first night we arrived he started thinking the whole idea of settling in America was a mistake.

There was an older white man just behind us in line. He spoke to us in Marathi, asking how he could help. He saw us through the customs line. He was a professor of Indian Studies at Berkeley, a widower with a large house. In those days we didn't have cell phones and we didn't have American money, and Ma didn't speak much English, so we'd have to trust someone. So we trusted the professor and followed him home.

If I hadn't been there—? But of course she didn't, and the professor was able to find my father's name and address and to drive us down to the house he'd bought on Camino Real.

I still cringe when I think of me, and my pride in that ridiculous red cowboy hat. I wore it every day. I thought it made me American and would help me learn English faster. Then a kid in my new neighbourhood called me stupid and knocked it off my head and trampled it on the sidewalk.

And now all those humiliating memories are crowding in. I'm sitting in the outer room, waiting for Pram to be wheeled back up. Waiting for Ma to find her way to the hospital. Borya is gone.

I'm fourteen, in the shower, soaping up, about to do what teenage boys do in the shower and suddenly she's there, pulling off her sleeping shirt and panties.

She's ten, and barely starting to be a woman. "Wash that soap off, please," she says. Then she puts her hands around it. "Way bigger than I figured." No need to explain why.

"What do you think you're doing?" I say, and she shrugs her naked shoulders and in that matter-of-fact way she looks up and says, "So this is the meaning of 'cocksucker'. The girls I know only have baby brothers. They're so wrong."

I must confess there were other times initiated by me. I don't feel good about them but I think of them now as inevitable. She always acted like an older woman, especially around me. I was always the boy, and she was the young lady. And there have been times when I wondered: is she using me? She's always been ten steps ahead of anyone in the room. So if a ten-year-old Indian girl is not a virgin, what's the purpose of dragging her back to India to save her virtue at twelve? She'd already made herself unsuited for an arranged marriage. Could she have been reading our father's intentions way back then?

When Pram was eleven, she published a paper on imaginary binary numbers in a Stanford mathematics journal. Then she "proved" a theorem in some other journal. When she was twelve she was racing through the Stanford undergraduate math courses on-line, and now I learn—just from watching her behaviour in the front seat—she's practically settling down with her ice-skating coach. And finally, I learn it might all be over for all of us. She has her survival algorithm. Our father made her take the ice-skating, just like he'd made me take up tennis, to be "more balanced," to "fit in," be really to show Americans that Indians could be champion athletes.

We're "fitting in" all right. We're very balanced. What's the algorithm for two Indo-Americans finding two Russian lovers?

For the next few weeks, I'm in Palo Alto at least as much as Santa Cruz. Pram is bald, but ties creative knots and twists with scarves and headbands, and she's feeling stronger. She's tolerating the course of treatment. "Remission" isn't mentioned, not just yet, but it seems likely. Ma is relieved, especially relieved that Dad, still waiting for that big, life-changing job, has kept his insurance payments up. He hasn't been told a thing.

On my own, would I have guessed that Ma was no longer our quiet, put-upon, librarian mother, but someone's mistress? I might have. The new shade of lipstick and the careful mascara are signs of life beyond the library. Those signs, and the fact that she doesn't mention Dad and his troubles. Those, and the fact that in two months she's suddenly collected more American lady friends than she's ever had, and that she "goes out with friends" for shopping or lunch or a movie. Dad had better stay in Mumbai.

These up-and-down trips are taking a toll. I've had to cut

classes, and I've missed a ton of practices. The coaching staff knows my predicament and they're behind me—to a point. But the tennis season has started, and looming out there is Mike Mahulkar. But one morning I get a text message from the Athletic Director himself. I am being summoned to his office, immediately.

But when I get to the outer ring of offices, the secretaries seem to be avoiding me. They don't look up from their computer screens. "In there," one says, and it's not even the door to the Assistant's Director's office. It's some kind of storage-room, with many boxes, two chairs and a table. Sitting there is a small-ish, middle-aged, turbaned Sikh in a blue jacket. Standing behind him is a second young man, Asian of some sort. Good news, I think: these guys can't drop my scholarship or kick me off the team. The Sikh stands and turns around and I see the letters ICE inscribed on his back. He tells me, maybe in Hindi, to take the other seat across from him. His name is—big surprise—Officer Singh. The other officer identifies himself as Mr. Soong.

He asks me something else, in Hindi. I don't understand, I and tell him so.

"I am asking, are you knowing what ICE means? Means 'Immigration and Customs Enforcement'. It is my duty to inform you that you are under detention as an undocumented alien. Unless you have new evidence of legal residence, you are to be deported."

"That's ridiculous," I say.

He responds, "It is law."

"I've been here since I was three years old!"

"That means fifteen years, illegally. Put hands in front." And when I do, Officer Soong clamps a plastic handcuff on my wrists. "Now we go to detention centre in Richmond—"

"What did I do? What are the charges?"

"—you meet immigration judge in the morning. You may choose to select a pro-bono immigration lawyer. It's Friday, so they may not be available till Monday. Then you'll spend an extra two days in detention. Pro-bono lawyers never win a case. Detention cells not good places."

"Then I want a regular lawyer."

"Immigration cases not covered by Constitutional rights. You have no right to lawyer or any of that other television rubbish."

I finally gather the courage to ask, "What is this all about?"

"I am arrest and transportation officer only. I have not seen papers or documents. Those are with judge. You are adult of eighteen years in this country without papers. You may reapply for readmission after ten years in your country of origin, meaning India."

"Let me make a phone call."

"Phone call not allowed. Already late." I ask for the list of pro-bono lawyers, looking for an Indian name, but there are none. I'm driven back up the peninsula in a detention van with four neck-tattooed gang-bangers, through San Francisco, over the Golden Gate and another bridge, past San Quentin. Richmond is one of those towns in the Bay Area that any sensible person avoids at night or certain areas by day, that Indians avoid at all times, a town we read about, full of gangs and street killings.

And then I'm processed, meaning that my cell phone, wallet, belt, keys and pen are confiscated for my night in detention. I have fifteen cellmates for eight beds, all Spanish-speaking, all joking, all laughing and playing cards. They look at me and can't quite decide what I am; maybe one of them, maybe not. I can't answer their questions, so I'm something else and they hold it against me—with unconfiscated knives—that I'm not one of them. They say, *oh, Palo Alto. Rich boy. Your mama can pay us. She don't want nothin bad happen her little boy. Your mama a good-lookin woman?* I make up an address and phone number. As they circle the cell they make sure to push off against my chest. If they allow a call, it should go to Arvind, to get the university involved. Or maybe Pram could get Borya to intervene. Maybe Borya's illegal, too.

When I meet the judge on Saturday morning, after shivering all night in my T-shirt and flip-flops, I'm ready to concede. I have no evidence; I just trusted too much. I'm like my father: I don't want to stay in this damned country. I don't care if Mike Mahulkar wins or loses. I don't care who's fucking my mother. I only care that my sister lives. The judge's name is Lourdes

Sanchez. It's one of those names I'll never forget. "Look," I say, "I'm on scholarship to UC-Santa Cruz. I've never broken a law."

We're joined by a young man holding a folder. I realize he's some sort of low-grade prosecutor or maybe just a clerk, but what he's holding in that manila folder is my future. Judge Sanchez introduces him as Mr. Powell.

"Is your counsel here?" he asks.

"I'm a freshman in college. I don't have a lawyer. I wasn't even allowed to make a phone call."

The judge says, "Immigration courts do not grant Constitutional favours, Mr. Waldekar. Count One, Mr. Powell?"

"Do you stipulate that you are a student at UC Santa Cruz?"

"Of course."

"And you are there on an athletic scholarship? Total value approximately $15,000?"

"I guess."

"You admit, then, defrauding the taxpayers of California for admission as a California resident?"

"I am a California resident."

"You cannot be a legal California resident if you are not a legal American resident."

The judge intervenes. "*Are* you a legal American resident, Mr. Waldekar? If you have evidence, this case is over. Fail to prove it, and it is also over."

I tell her I'm not deceitful. My mother is a Permanent Resident, my sister is a natural-born citizen and my father is a naturalized citizen although he's temporarily in India; how could they leave me unprotected? I was an American kid in a cowboy hat, what did I know? I never asked if they'd fixed my citizenship—I just assumed. I tell her that my sister is in remission from leukaemia, but if she falls out of remission in the next three years I am a compatible transplant donor, and on top of that, she is a national treasure, the youngest undergraduate in Stanford history.

And the judge says, "The Immigration Act under which I operate does not permit exemption from deportation on grounds of blood compatibility, or for exceptionally high IQs. I will drop the charges related to your scholarship—the University did not exercise due diligence. The Immigration Act is eminently fair.

You might be a college boy on a tennis scholarship from a middle-class home in Palo Alto, and the gentlemen you spent the night with might be despicable street thugs in your eyes, but you are all equal in the eyes of this Act. You are no different than farm workers or busboys or housepainters. There are millions of your people now in America, and I'm certain that another donor for your sister can be found."

"They can't," I say, but my voice is crumbling.

"Mr. Powell," she says, "this Court is prepared to render a verdict." Powell clicks his pen. "Mr. Waldekar will be deported to New Delhi in all haste."

And then she leans across the bench to address me personally. "This will sound harsh. I will not open up an avenue—blood compatibility with your national treasure of a sister—to an exemption that is not contemplated in the Act. I will not expose my court to superior review. I will not challenge a national law for the sake of one undocumented alien. Are you prepared for the verdict?"

She straightens up, clears her throat, and speaks to Mr. Powell. "Mr. Waldekar is not represented by counsel. He has not disputed the government case against him. His pleas of innocence have no credibility." She shifts her vision to me. "Therefore, without credible challenge to the documents provided to me, I find your immigration status to be in violation of the law. You have assumed rights and privileges of a legal resident. Indeed, in numerous documents you have claimed American citizenship. There is a flight to Buffalo tonight, and you will be put on it, and in the morning you will be placed on a direct flight to New Delhi. Since you are innocent of outstanding warrants, you may travel unescorted. You do not have an Indian passport, or that of any other country; so Indian authorities will be notified, unless of course you want to be returned to your cell. In ten years, you may re-apply for entry-consideration to an immigration panel, provided you have no outstanding warrants, judgments, arrests or convictions. Your situation is no different from judgments I pass every day, sending apparently American children to countries they've never visited, and into languages they've never spoken. Somehow, they all survive."

"Do they?" I try to ask, but my mouth is dry and my tongue

sticks to the roof of my mouth. I want to say, do you have direct evidence of their survival? I want to say, who benefits from this? I swallow hard, and my tongue is free.

Down the hall I hear someone sobbing, then the voices come closer and grow louder, and I make out cursing, and screaming obscenities, and from the corner of my eye I see two officers get off their chairs and move toward me, unclipping Tasers from their belts.

VALERIE SPENCER has directed community planning for several departments of municipal government and served on the faculties of two universities, but took early retirement to work at creative writing. Born in Ontario, she has made her home for many years in Nova Scotia, where she is also active in music and visual arts.

CAROLINE ADDERSON is the author of three novels and two collections of stories. Her work has received numerous award nominations including the Giller Prize, the Governor General's Award, the Rogers' Trust Fiction Prize and the Commonwealth Writers' Prize, and she is a two-time winner of the Ethel Wilson Fiction Prize and three-time winner of the CBC Literary Award.

MARJORIE CELONA is the author of the novel *Y*. Her short stories have appeared in *The Best American Nonrequired Reading, Harvard Review, Glimmer Train, The Fiddlehead* and elsewhere. Born and raised on Vancouver Island, she lives in Cincinnati.

KATHRYN MULVIHILL was born in Ottawa and moved to Cole Harbour and Whitby as a child before returning to Ottawa to attend Carleton University. She lives with her husband in Cantley, Quebec, and is a member of Mary Borsky's writing workshop in Ottawa. This is her first publication.

ALICE PETERSEN grew up in New Zealand. Her stories have been published in *Takahe, Geist, Fiddlehead* and *Room*, and shortlisted for the Journey Prize, the Writers' Union of Canada Competition and the CBC Literary Award. Petersen lives in Shawinigan with her husband and two daughters. Her first collection, *All the Voices Cry*, appeared in 2012.

PATRICIA ROBERTSON has been nominated for the National Magazine Awards (three times), the Journey Prize and the Pushcart Prize. Her most recent collection is *The Goldfish Dancer*. Her previous collection, *City of Orphans*, was nominated for the Ethel Wilson Fiction Prize.

HEATHER DAVIDSON graduated from Concordia University, where she won the Irving Layton Fiction Award. Her work has appeared in *The New Quarterly, Descant* and *Contemporary Verse 2*. "The Fires of Soweto" is dedicated to the memory of her father, Dan James Davidson, 1956-2013.

ELISABETH DE MARIAFFI has published widely in Canadian magazines and her first collection of stories, *How To Get Along With Women*, was longlisted for the Giller Prize. One of the original minds behind Toronto Poetry Vendors, a small press that sells single poems by established Canadian poets through $2 vending machines, she is now based in St. John's.

ZOEY LEIGH PETERSON has published fiction in various literary journals including *The Malahat Review, Grain* and *PRISM international*. "Sleep World" originally appeared in *The New Quarterly*, and won the Peter Hinchcliffe Fiction Award. She lives in Vancouver, where she is working on a novel.

CYNTHIA FLOOD has published a novel and four books of short fiction, the most recent of which is *Red Girl Rat Boy*. Her stories have been widely anthologized and have won both a National Magazine Award and the Journey Prize. She lives in Vancouver.

CLARK BLAISE recently published his tenth book of stories, *The Meagre Tarmac*. All the stories in that collection are narrated from Indo-Canadian or Indo-American points-of-view—Blaise has been married to Bharati Mukherjee for 47 years. In 2010 he was named to the Order of Canada. Now retired from teaching, he lives in San Francisco.

JOHN METCALF is one of Canada's best-known editors. He was born in England in 1938, emigrated to Montreal in 1962 and currently lives in Ottawa with his wife Myrna. In 2004 he was made a member of the Order of Canada. His most recent books are *Shut Up He Explained*, a memoir, and *Standing Stones*, a collection of selected stories.